YSOBELLA BLACK

THE ICE MAIDEN & THE PRINCES OF DIAMONDS

FAIRY TALES WITH A KINK: STORY 2 - MFM BDSM

Table of Contents

WORKS BY THE AUTHOR

All of my stories and series, except for Alix in Wonderland and Raven Chronicles, are a different aspect of my Dragaverse, but can be read and enjoyed as standalone.

Stories by Ysobel Black (Nice/Sweet Versions)

Bakery Street Cozy Mysteries

Paranormal Cozy Mysteries
The Lyrical Lycanthrope

Fairy Tales With a Twist

Retellings of fairy tales, myths, and stories you only thought you knew.
The Crimson Hood & the Alpha of Wolves
The Ice Maiden & the Princes of Diamonds

Holiday Hullabaloo

Love in Ashana can be tricky, but twelve days of chaos result in paranormal happily-ever-afters.
A Penghou in a Pine Tree
Two Tatzelwurms
Three French Bêtes
Four Ceffyl Dŵr
Five Golden Wings

Six Grootslangs Playing
Seven Spawns a-Swimming
Eight Maenads Mixing
Nine Lazy Dragons
Ten Swords a-Sneaking
Eleven Pixie Potions
Twelve Lovers Loving

Pohjola Maidens

The Maidens of Pohjola are free, heading for the human world, and looking for love.
Dream's Sleeper: Lemminki

Strygoi Witches & Vampires

Join an Ildum of vampires over 10,000 years of history and mythology as they find their Dragăs — witches who make their hearts beat and restore their souls.
Ember's Light: Stryx
Viktoria's Shadow: Jael
Myth's Legend: Norrix
Bijou's Cure: Zeke
Musette's Fate: Idris

Strygoi Witches & Vampires Companion Stories

Shadowy — Viktoria's prequel (companion novella)
Echo's Answer: Lachlan (companion novel)

COLLECTIONS/BOX SETS

Holiday Hullabaloo
DAYS 1-12

Strygoi Witches & Vampires
COLLECTION ONE, BOOKS 1-4

Stories by Ysobella Black
(Naughty/Steamy Versions)

Alix in Wonderland

A reverse harem (MFMMM) retelling of Alice in Wonderland.
Madness of the Hatter

Bakery Street Mysteries

Paranormal Cozy-ish Mysteries
The Lyrical Lycanthrope

Fairy Tales With a Kink

Retellings of fairy tales, myths, and stories you only thought you knew.
The Crimson Hood & the Alpha of Wolves
The Ice Maiden & the Princes of Diamonds

Grove of Bandrui

Immortal Druids search for their Maités.
Druid of Oaks
Druid of Apples

Harom & Aneja

Witches choose three men to form their Haroms as they become
Aneja — Walkers in magic. Reverse Harem (MFMM)
RealmWalker
BeastWalker

Magical Love in London

Regency London with a Paranormal twist
A Marriage of Inconvenience

Oubliette

Paranormal Short and Steamy Stories
Selkie
Merrow

Pohjola Passions

The Maidens of Pohjola are free, heading for the human world, and
looking for love.
Dream's Sleeper: Lemminki

Raven Chronicles: Phoenix Rising

An epic spanning generations — the battle for the Raven Throne is
full of sex, intrigue, and betrayal.
First Generation

Souls Lost & Found

Under a Blue Moon, star-crossed lovers get a second chance for their love to shine.
The Egyptian

Utopia Pack Shifters

A pack of shifters find their Fateds.
Unyielding

Vampires & Strygoi Witches

Join an Ildum of vampires over 10,000 years of history and mythology as they find their Dragăs — witches who make their hearts beat and restore their souls.
Ember's Light: Stryx
Viktoria's Shadow: Jael
Myth's Legend: Norrix
Bijou's Cure: Zeke
Musette's Fate: Idris

Vampires & Strygoi Witches Companion Stories

Shadowy — Viktoria's Prequel (Companion Novella)
Echo's Answer: Lachlan (Companion Novel)

Xuterias: Xov & Xau

Enemies to Lovers Paranormal Romances
Poisoned Heart

Yuletide Chaos

Short Paranormal Romances about finding love in mystical Ashana.
A Penghou in a Pine Tree
Two Tatzelwurms
Three French Bêtes
Four Ceffyl Dŵr
Five Golden Wings
Six Grootslangs Playing
Seven Spawns a-Swimming
Eight Maenads Mixing
Nine Lazy Dragons
Ten Swords a-Sneaking
Eleven Pixie Potions
Twelve Lovers Loving
12 Days of Chaos Box Set

COLLECTIONS/BOX SETS

Three First in a Series

FATED – Three Firsts

Ember's Light:Stryx
RealmWalker
Poisoned Heart

Five First in a Series

<u>FATED – Five Firsts</u>
Ember's Light:Stryx
The Crimson Hood & the Alpha of Wolves
RealmWalker
Dream's Sleeper: Lemminki
Poisoned Heart

<u>Vampires & Strygoi Witches</u>
<u>COLLECTION ONE: BOOKS 1-4</u>

<u>Yuletide Yearnings</u>
DAYS 1-12

<u>https://ysobellablack.com/newsletter</u>[1]

---

1. https://ysobellablack.com/newsletter/

FRIDAY,

DECEMBER 13

CHAPTER ONE

FROSTINE

FROSTINE HELD HER BREATH and willed the floorboards not to creak as she crept down the hallway. When her stepmother was... *entertaining*, it was better to be out of the house. She hadn't expected the second visitor today.

Once there were thick runners and tapestries to muffle the sounds of anyone walking the corridors, but now only threadbare throw rugs lay on the old wooden planks. If they were worth anything, they would have been sold long before now.

The rhythmic moans and thumping behind her stepmother's closed door weren't surprising. Lady Prudence Collymoore used her body as currency, but the male voice carried an undertone of anger, even without being able to discern individual words.

Prudence was eager to curry favor. It wasn't like her to argue with the men who offered the power she wanted to wield. The sound of a hand smacking flesh and a strangled cry froze Frostine in place. Was this different than her stepmother's usual encounters? Did she need help?

"Well, well, well, what do we have here? A voyeur?"

Frostine's head snapped up and she screamed. A fat man wearing only underwear loomed in front of her. His hairy chest and belly jiggled as he stepped toward her, reeking of sour wine.

Sounds from the bedroom stopped.

The fat man grabbed her arm, pulled her to his sweaty body, and covered her mouth with a musty smelling, slick palm, holding her against him. His other hand groped her. Material ripped as he pawed at her bodice and pinched her breasts.

"Where has dear Prudence been hiding you, sweetling?"

Frostine snapped out of her terrified paralysis and nearly wrenched herself free, but he hauled her back with his disgusting hand covering her mouth again, and opened her stepmother's bedroom door.

It was the largest room in the house, and contained the most expensive furnishings, all the ones that remained, from the thick woven carpets scattered over the wooden floor, to colorful tapestries on the walls, and heavy wooden furniture polished to a shine. Prudence lay on her four-poster bed, chest down, backside up. Makeup smeared over her flushed face, and her usually perfectly coiffed hair was a wild tangle.

A second naked pudgy man knelt behind her. He held her head in place by her long brown hair wrapped in his fist. The man smacked Prudence's rear hard, leaving a red handprint on her flesh. "You've been holding out on us, Prudence?" He spanked her again. "That's no way to get an invitation to meet the Prince."

"Not holding out," Prudence murmured in a throaty voice. "Saving. No one at court has set eyes on her since she was a child. Introduce me to the Prince, and you can have her first."

Have her? First? Frostine stiffened. No. Her stepmother never liked her, but surely she wouldn't...

"We could have her now." The man gripping Frostine slid his free hand up her front to squeeze her breast.

Frostine bit into the gross fingers covering her mouth. The man swore and shoved her. She stumbled forward, her face slamming into the bedpost. She bounced off, and tore herself free. Her molester reached for her again, but panic made her fleet, and she sprinted out of the room.

Clutching the torn pieces of her bodice together, Frostine dashed down the stairs, snatched a cloak from the closet, and flung the front door open. Tears blurring her vision, she ran down the street. She dabbed a ragged sleeve at the blood trickling from her nose, not paying attention to where she walked.

The Enchanted City didn't feel magical today. The sparkling palace in the distance seemed less grand. The birdsong less chipper.

Her thin-soled slippers, meant for indoors only, scuffed along unforgiving pavement for block after block. Footsore, Frostine stepped into a park, the soft grass underfoot a welcome change. Her favorite bench stood empty, and she sank into the curved wooden seat gratefully.

This park was her first memory. The pond frozen over. Snow on the ground and dusting the tall evergreens. Mother and Father laughing with her, free with their hugs, kisses, and love.

How had everything gone so wrong? Once, she'd had two loving parents, then one, and now only a stepmother who had never cared for her. She remembered lavish parties, delicious meals, and new dresses. Now she lived in an empty house, wore threadbare clothing, and survived on bread.

She pulled her cloak around herself to hide the torn material. Even her skill with a needle might not be enough to repair the damage.

Frostine watched a swan swimming ahead of a row of ducklings. The birds recognized her as a frequent visitor and waddled from the water to gather around her feet. Had she planned to come here, she would have brought a crust or two for them.

"I'm sorry. I didn't bring anything this time."

The swan seemed to understand, and laid her head on Frostine's leg. Frostine stroked soft feathers. "What I wouldn't give to be able to fly away with you."

Intelligent, gentle, black eyes turned a sad gaze on her.

The birds kept her company until late afternoon gave way to sunset, when they took to the air. Frostine shivered as stars filled the sky. Her stepmother should have had enough time to finish with her...visitors by now.

Heavy feet carried Frostine back to her house. Or what should have been her house. It had belonged to her mother, not her father, and shouldn't have been part of any estate left to her stepmother. It didn't matter. Frostine had no money or anywhere else to go.

She turned onto her street. A crowd of blue-uniformed men gathered in front of her home. The City Guard? Had something happened? Guilt gnawed at her stomach. Had one of those men hurt Prudence? As nobles, they could do what they liked without worrying about consequences.

When she neared, one guard spotted her and pointed. "There she is!" The others turned, drew clubs from their belts and headed toward Frostine.

She turned to flee.

"You! Halt! You're under arrest for assault, battery, and prostitution."

Hands grabbed her, wrenching her arms behind her back. Cold metal closed around her wrists and they marched her toward a windowless carriage in front of her house. Prudence came out of the front door. Perfectly coiffed, she wore an expensive golden gown. She crossed her arms and her eyes glittered as she sashayed down the walkway and stopped in front of Frostine.

"But I'm not a prostitute! I was the one assaulted!" In desperation, Frostine turned to her stepmother. "Tell them!"

Prudence leaned in close. "You stupid, ungrateful girl. I was meant to be a queen, and you have brought me to this level of squalor. Did you think I would ever forgive you?" Her stepmother faced the city guards. "Take her." Fake tears ran down her cheeks. "I've done my best for her. She's beyond what I can deal with."

The guards bodily lifted Frostine as she struggled and locked her in their transport.

She kicked the side of the carriage. "Stop this! I'm not a prostitute! I didn't hurt anyone!" Couldn't they see the damage done to her face?

Someone outside hit the carriage hard enough to shake the entire thing. "Save it, girl."

Fear replaced rage.

What had she done to deserve this?

CHAPTER TWO

PRINCE CHARLES

ABOUT THE ONLY PERK of being the prince of a nearly bankrupt kingdom was the number of women who threw themselves at him. Two of said women lay in the bed, one on each side of him, sleeping off their exertions. These women were just looking for a romp, and were safe. They had no illusions about becoming a princess or a queen. The ones who did, he avoided like incurable contagious diseases. As far as he was concerned, that's what marriage was.

He blinked at the unfamiliar water-stained ceiling.

Their place, then, not one of his. Even a nearly bankrupt kingdom provided its prince with solid roofs and clean ceilings.

The home was small, but clean and well-tended. Charlie debated leaving the women some money, but he'd tried that before and it had backfired terrifically. He would send them gifts instead. Enough food for a month, maybe. His bed mates had beauty, but their thin frames were from hunger, not trying to keep up with the latest fashion. Hardly anyone had enough, but the palace always had extra.

Politics and entitlement. Ugh.

Charlie hated all of it, all the more since he could do nothing about providing jobs or food for the masses.

Yet.

One of the women stirred. Time to go.

He hated awkward goodbyes. He carefully lifted various arms and legs to clear the way and slipped out of the bed. Tiptoeing across the worn wooden floorboards, he stopped at randomly scattered clothing strewn across the floor and furniture.

Really, how many layers did one woman need to wear? Stockings, gowns, petticoats, shifts, drawers — and when he undressed two women, their discarded things seemed to multiply by themselves.

Charlie found his pants and pulled them on. Searched some more to find his shirt on the stairs, one boot in a potted tree, the other under a sofa. Scooping up his cloak from an armchair, he pulled the hood over his head and eased out the door, setting the latch so it locked behind him.

In the chill morning, he took a deep breath of fresh air and made his way through Enchanted City. This was his favorite time. No pressures. No expectations. No complaining. In the dawning light, it was easy to pretend the city was still rich. All its imperfections remained hidden in shadow and muted lighting. No houses that needed repairs. No cracked or potholed streets. No people with gaunt cheeks staring at him with hopeless eyes.

He glanced around to make sure he wasn't watched, and turned down an alley. In between the back doors of a butcher and a candlestick maker, the sign over the middle door read The Baker's Dozen. The door swung open silently on well-oiled hinges, but the shop had been abandoned. A hidden door at the back of a storeroom led to tunnels under the city, and merged into secret passages riddling the palace.

Taking the twists and turns by rote, Charlie pushed a wall panel aside and exited into his chambers. A shower was first on his agenda, to wash the scents of sex and perfume away. Changing into pajama pants, he wondered what form of torture his parents had lined up for him today.

The kingdom was already in dire straits when his father had taken over. The Alpha wars in the Foreboding Forest required the city to maintain a standing army. An expensive standing army. His father had poured his own money into the coffers in an effort to keep the kingdom safe and viable, but that couldn't continue much longer. Nobles kept their purses closed, and now a lot of them were richer than the king.

That never made things awkward.

With the threat of an arranged marriage, to whichever princess had the largest dowry, hanging over his head, Charlie desperately needed the diamond mine to give up its treasures. One spectacular find could save him from marriage, and the kingdom from ruin.

Time to contact his brother.

CHAPTER THREE

PRINCE DASHIELL

"BROTHER, BROTHER, WORKING the mine," the mirror on Dashiell's bedroom wall chanted.

Rolling over in bed, Dashiell glared at the looking glass, where his doppelgänger's face wavered into view. His twin's short, dark hair stood in spikes. Shadowy stubble dusted his jawline. Fine lines around his dark brown eyes could be exhaustion, but was worry, and his normally urbane voice held a note of worry.

"Tell me everything is fine," the mirror finished.

Dashiell laughed. Awful rhymes, inaccuracies, and irreverence annoyed the mirror magic. He and Charlie weren't exactly brothers. Not by blood, anyway. And the mirror preferred to be addressed rather than used as a conduit.

"Do you have any idea what time it is, Charming?"

The prince frowned like it was a truly perplexing question. "Uh, bedtime? Don't be mad, Dashing."

Dashiell yawned and sat up, sheets pooling around his hips. Charming rarely gave a thought to when others might be sleeping even before he was a prince. He acted on impulse whenever an impulse struck.

Pale moonlight streamed through the narrow gap in the curtains. No point in going back to sleep now. The trolls would be showing up to work. They lived for swinging pick axes at rocks.

But there wasn't great news. "Fine is one word, I suppose. We've extracted a number of diamonds, but there aren't any huge finds at the moment."

"Are you saying the mine is played out?" Strain marred his brother's normally playful, unflappable face. The Enchanted City was on the edge of bankruptcy. The mine and the work were important. If there were no more diamonds, the monarchy was ruined.

Having to maintain a constantly ready army because of the Alpha wars happening in the Foreboding Forest was expensive, and generated no revenue.

Dashiell had the good luck to stumble on the mine when he led a contingent to maintain the buffer between the Alphas and the rest of the world. After a few significant finds, hopes were high the kingdom could be financially saved.

"No. It's not played out. There are still diamonds. But we've found seams of new gemstones we need to get through first. We need more workers if all you need is diamonds quickly. Even seven rock trolls can only do so much."

Charming blew out a sigh of relief. "All right. I'll see what I can do. Let me know if anything changes." He squinted into the mirror. "You look like crap. You should get some sleep."

His smirking face disappeared.

Dashiell rolled his eyes. Ever since his startling resemblance to Charming was discovered when they were boys, his life had no longer been his own. Taken from his parents to live in the palace, his life should have been a dream, but he was never himself. He always had to think of what the prince would say, what action the prince would take. Act like he could stand the prince's friends, and was attracted to the women the prince preferred, going so far as to share them.

The only time he was in control was in the privacy of his own bedroom — and there he demanded total submission from his bed partners.

Dashiell sighed.

Not that there were any women here. He needed to finish this project.

If riches were so important to the royal family, it seemed like they'd send enough men to work the cursed mine that provided the wealth. Granted work at the mine was dangerous, but surely they'd make their money back, even if they had to offer higher wages.

Even without the inherently risky work, just being on the land was perilous. The mine was in disputed territory, in both the Dark Forest so it was always night, and the Foreboding Forest, where it was always winter. Wolves raiding the area, plus the constant dark and freezing temperatures weren't exactly enticing lures.

He glanced out the window at the trees. He didn't want to be here, either.

SUNDAY,
DECEMBER 15

CHAPTER FOUR

FROSTINE

FROSTINE WEPT, ALLOWING this weakness once every day. Or at least her best guess at when a day passed. So far, she'd cried twice. She leaned against the slimy, cold wall, an apathetic trickle of water sliding down her back. Her face ached, and one eye had swollen nearly shut.

She'd never expected her stepmother to do this. It didn't seem real. Was Prudence really just going to leave her here?

There had been no explanations or appearances in court. No offers to take a bribe for her freedom. Not that she could have paid a bribe, but it would have been hope there was a way out of the darkness. All that interrupted the monotony was the bowl of rotten smelling slop in a bowl they slid into the cell with her a couple of times a day.

A key rattled in the lock. Frostine swiped at her wet eyes as the door swung open. Bright light blinded her when a guard thrust a flaming torch into the small cell. "Get up, whore."

Frostine found she could still laugh, albeit the sound escaping her as a slightly hysterical giggle. She had tried sex and decided she wasn't missing anything. Not to mention, she was here because she refused to sell herself and fought against being raped!

Not that anyone believed her. Frostine climbed to her feet, swaying with light-headedness. She hadn't been eating the food. It was moldy and disgusting. A rough hand grabbed her arm and propelled her down a dark corridor into a room that smelled like damp and soap.

"Hurry up and make yourself presentable." The guard placed the torch in a wall bracket and left her alone.

The idea of a bath almost sent her into tears again, but for an entirely different reason.

Invisible hands tore her ragged clothes away and tossed buckets of water at her from every direction. It was tepid, but clear and sweet-smelling. Bristled brushes foamed as they scrubbed her filthy skin. She forced her embarrassment away and relished being clean. When the unseen hands moved to wash her unkempt tangle of hair, she almost thought maybe she'd died in the filthy cell, and this was heaven.

All too soon, the respite was over, and a scratchy towel rubbed her skin.

The door opened and the guard laughed as she tried to cover herself. He tossed a bit of white material at her. "Put that on if it'll make you feel better."

He spun and headed out the door.

Frostine held up the soft material. Normally something so silky would feel decadent, but it was sheer and would hide nothing of her body. A sinking feeling opened in the pit of her stomach. She didn't need this scrap of finery to return to her cell, but if they really thought she was a prostitute...

"Put that on and move, or just move," the guard called. "Makes no difference to me if you wear it or not, you're going either way."

Going where? She gulped. Maybe the gown was better than nothing. Frostine slid it over her head. It swished around her thighs as she hurried out of the wash room.

He led her into a cavern where more women stood in a line, each wearing a different color skimpy nightgown — hers white, one dark gold, another the yellow-orange of sunshine, one gray, a pink, and a woman wearing orange.

Several figures wore long black robes with hoods pulled over their heads. They moved with more guards among the women.

"Here's the last one." The guard shoved her forward.

Frostine stumbled to her place at the end of the row.

"So few?" a gravelly voice rumbled from one of the hooded robes.

"We've already emptied the jails." A burly guard ran his finger down the arm of the woman wearing gray. She snarled at him and he flinched. "These are all new arrests. Fresh and young. We'll let you have them for a fair price."

A sinking sensation threatened to swallow her. Slavers. The guards were going to sell her.

One black-robed slaver grabbed Frostine's chin and tilted her face up, turning her head to the side in the torchlight. "This one is damaged."

"She came in that way. We didn't touch her."

"Discount this one twenty percent and we'll take them all. It's not like their new men won't mark them up." He laughed.

Several of the women gasped.

A slaver threw something at the floor and a portal swirled in the air. On the other side, a dense forest awaited. Frostine's eyes widened and she took a step back only to be shoved forward. With all those snow-covered, crooked, dark trees, that had to be the Foreboding Forest! Four more hooded figures awaited their arrival.

Frostine took another step backward. They couldn't mean to dress her like this and send her there!

Rough hands shoved her through the gateway. Frostine stumbled into the magic. Her stomach swirled in nauseating lurches as the portal transported her to the most dangerous place she'd ever heard of.

Snow crunched under her bare feet as she careened out of the gateway. She took a deep breath of crisp, icy air, only realizing now how stale and oppressive the atmosphere in the dungeon was. Despite the stark wintry landscape, a small part of her felt like she'd come home. Sheer joy filled her soul and she lifted her arms to twirl.

Mocking laughter reminded her of her precarious situation.

What was she thinking? She'd be killed here! It was full of the worst kinds of people!

Frostine spun back to the glowing doorway, the sight of the dank prison on the other side. It was safer in the dungeon! She lunged for the portal.

Hands grabbed her, and she couldn't help herself. Frostine kicked, shrieked, and fought, but more of the hooded figures seized her arms and legs.

"Get that one bound and gagged," a man ordered. "She'll bring the Crimson Hood down on our heads."

Frostine struggled with a strength she had never possessed before. A flailing elbow smashed into a nose. Her bare feet kicked into knees and softer flesh.

"She's one woman!" someone snapped. "Get her under control!"

A man tackled her, pinning her to the snow under his heavy bulk. Two more slavers locked manacles around her wrists.

"Let me go!" She swung her manacles at the nearest face.

Three women stumbled through the portal. They saw her predicament, then raced into the forest. "No! Help me. Please!"

Slavers cursed and ran into the woods after the escapees.

The last of the women came through.

"Help, please!"

A couple of the women looked regretful, but darted away and disappeared into the trees.

Frostine gasped as a boot thudded into her stomach.

She was on her own. Frostine redoubled her fight.

Gruff voices swore and hard fingers dug into her skin.

"This one's already marked up, and too much trouble. We'll sell her to Fagin and find the rest."

More boots and a few fists impacted her body. Frostine screamed until a hand closed around her throat. Her cry cut off along with her air. Stars flashed in her vision and everything went black.

MONDAY,
DECEMBER 16

CHAPTER FIVE

FROSTINE

FROSTINE SURFACED FROM darkness to pain and... Hallucination.

A line of four women and three men, all short, gray-skinned, silver-haired, and pointy-eared, with big, black eyes stood alongside the small bed she lay on.

The tallest, who might reach Frostine's elbow, was a curvy woman with a long braid. Roundest of them was a man with a short haircut and trim beard. One couldn't control his giggles, wild hair sticking up in all directions. A woman couldn't meet Frostine's eyes, hiding her face in her curtain of long curls. Beside her, a man with a bushy beard made his equally bushy eyebrows meet on his forehead as he frowned. The next woman grinned, tucking her shiny chin-length hair behind her ears.

Finally, a woman wore round glasses and a severe bun cleared her throat and stepped forward. "The slavers did a number on you. They didn't break any bones, but you'll be sore for a few days. We've got some whiskey, but no medicine. We might be able to get some in the morning. The overseer is a bastard, but the man in charge overall is reasonable."

"Where am I?" Her head throbbed. Frostine touched a lump on the back of her skull. Her whole body ached, and her sides hurt when she breathed.

The room was some sort of dormitory. Seven empty beds, made of stone platforms, all neatly made with pillows and blankets. The ceiling and walls were constructed of stone, but the place felt homey rather than stark.

"What happened?" Frostine rubbed her neck. It hurt to talk. Like her throat was too narrow to let the words out.

"Slavers caught you." The frowning man smiled. "Apparently, you gave them some trouble, and they sold you to the Overseer for, um, to work in the mine. We snuck you to our house."

"Try to drink some water." The smiling woman held a cup to Frostine's lips.

Cool water soothed her throat, but made her shiver.

"Here." The giggling man tucked a blanket around her shoulders. "You're small. We have some spare clothes that will almost fit you, unless you want to, um, keep wearing that."

Frostine glanced down at the sheer white nightgown, now ripped and stained with blood and dirt. "I'd rather not wear this anymore, if it's all the same to you."

The bespectacled woman nodded and laid out an assortment of clothes on the bed. "You can choose what works best. We'll give you some privacy. Meet us in the main room when you're ready and you can get some food into you. We're going to have an after midnight snack."

They filed out and closed the door.

A pair of pants had to be tied at the waist with a rope for a belt, the cuffs leaving half her shins bare. The shirt billowed around her, sleeves nearly at her elbows. A too tight leather vest served to keep her breasts in place, if a bit squished. The socks fit well enough, as did a spare pair of boots that were only a little too big.

Dressed, Frostine ducked through the low doorway into a combination parlor, dining room, and kitchen. Seven pickaxes hung in a neat row on the wall near the door. A fragrant pot of stew bubbled from its hook in the fireplace, and eight place settings were arranged on a long table.

The roundest troll brought the stew to the table, then detoured into the small kitchen. An aroma of fresh, warm bread wafted through the cozy house, almost bringing Frostine to tears.

When had she last eaten? Must have been days ago.

She sat at the place the bespectacled troll indicated and refrained from gorging herself as one by one everyone was served.

"Thank you for helping me." These strangers were the only ones who had shown her kindness since her father died. "My name is Frostine. Who are all of you?"

"Our names are too hard for humans to say, and you think they all sound the same." The tallest troll dipped her bread into her stew. "We can usually figure out who you're talking to."

Frostine lifted her spoon to her lips and savored the meaty stew on her tongue. "This is delicious."

"Thank you." The roundest troll beamed. Frostine mentally named him Stout.

"We're in the Foreboding Forest aren't we? What are all of you doing here?"

Their answers came a little at a time as they went around the table.

"This is technically the Dark Forest, on the border of the Foreboding Forest. So it's just dark all the time rather than winter. And no Alphas." Smiley was clearly the optimist of the group.

"We're miners." Spectacles pointed at the axes on the wall. "It's the only work we can find since the Alphas took over the Foreboding Forest. We don't want to work for them. It's not the cleanest or safest job, but it's the only way we get to keep what we rightfully earn."

"We'll do our best to keep you safe." A flush crept up Shy's cheeks as she twisted coils of long curls around her fingers.

"We're rock trolls, and it's good work. When we're finished with this mine, we'll be rich enough to retire." Statuesque, the tallest, rubbed her hands together.

"We were chosen because we can fit into small places. And have a canny sense of where the gems are." Silly tapped his nose and giggled. "That's our magic."

"Plus, it's pretty much the only work we can get, what with Alphas rampaging everywhere." Scowly frowned. "The Foreboding Forest was our home first, and they ran us out. If there's a way we can help the King's army win, we're going to do it."

A fist pounded on the door, and a tall man with cruel eyes stomped into the house without waiting for anyone to open the door. Vivid scars on his cheek pulled as he sneered. "That," he pointed a thick finger at her, "doesn't belong to you, trolls."

"She doesn't belong to you, either, Fagin." Scowly snarled.

"I paid for the whore."

"I'm *not* a whore." Everyone ignored her. All seven trolls glared at Fagin.

"You used funds for the mine to pay for her, so she belongs to the royal family, if anyone." Spectacles tilted her head. "How do they feel about buying people? Oh yes. They disapprove."

Fagin laughed. "You think we can't take her from you? We bought the whore for the good of the mine. Morale for the men."

Frostine shuddered, but didn't bother protesting. No one listened anyway.

"Back off, Fagin." Scowly put a growl into his voice. "She's injured."

"Not too injured to lay on her back."

Frostine gasped and jumped to her feet. She would stab him with her spoon if she had to.

The trolls formed a line in front of her, seeming much larger than their small statures should allow. "You hold no sway here, nor are you welcome." Scowly took a step forward, fists balled.

"For now." Fagin's empty eyes flicked from troll to troll. "You all work for me, just like everyone else. We'll see how things go tomorrow. She'll have to work. No freeloaders taking up space and eating food." He ran his eyes over her in a way that made her feel naked. "You don't look like a miner to me."

"I'll work." Frostine straightened, trying not to wince as her ribs sent sharp pain through her.

Fagin leered at her and licked his lips.

She raised her chin. "In the mine."

His lust morphed into rage. "We'll see how long that lasts." He slammed the door as he stormed out.

A shaky breath escaped her, and Frostine pressed a hand to her sore ribs as she sank into her seat.

Smiley patted her hand. "Try to get some sleep. You're safe with us tonight."

Frostine hoped that statement was based on more than optimism and tried to rest.

Far too soon she woke to gentle jostling.

"Time to get up."

Frostine sat up and yawned. "It feels so early."

"It will take some time to get used to waking up in the dark. Breakfast helps." Stout pressed a slice of bread and some cheese into Frostine's hands. "It's easier to retrain our stomachs."

She pulled on her too big boots and ate on the short hike, entering an echoey cavern after a few minutes. The rock trolls helped her when she stumbled in the gloominess. One main chamber separated into several tunnels.

"We're working down here today." Spectacles pointed to the farthest passage on the left, lit with faint blue lights that floated near the ceiling.

Frostine tried not to think about the dank dungeon where she'd been a prisoner. There was light here, and she wasn't alone. She hefted a spare pick axe the trolls found for her, and turned to follow them.

Fagin's unpleasant, scarred face leered down at her as she passed him. "Hi, whore. Off to work you go."

"I'm not a whore." Frostine was getting tired of explaining that.

"Work on your back, or work in the mine."

"I said I would work in the mine." Frostine hefted her pick axe. "That's where we're going."

He snorted. "We'll see how long that lasts."

The day turned into a monotony of movement.

Lift the pick axe.

Swing it down.

Lift the pick axe.

Swing it down.

Her muscles and injuries ached. Blisters formed on her hands.

Farther up the tunnel, the trolls argued with Fagin. It wasn't the first time they'd disagreed with him that day.

"You trolls aren't finding anything," the overseer complained. "The spell will! Then we'll at least know where to look."

"You can't force rock to your will!"

"The witch said it would work!" Fagin waved a vial around.

"Use it on the rock between your ears!" a troll yelled. "It's too dangerous. We've got to extract the sapphires and rubies before we get to the next seam of diamonds. It'll be worth it even if it takes longer."

"We don't have the time."

"We don't have the men! Give us today. See how far we get. Then we can use the magic when everyone is out."

"Today." Fagin stomped off.

Six of the trolls spread out and tapped on the walls with their pick axes, tilting their heads to listen. That must be how their magic worked.

Spectacles took the axe from Frostine's hands. "Why don't you take a break and get some water? There's a barrel in the main chamber where we came in. Do you think you can find it?"

Frostine nodded and trudged wearily through the tunnels. She joined a short line and drank cool, fresh water from a ladle when it was her turn, then filled a canteen to take back for the others.

Moving automatically, she followed the green lights, trusting her feet to take her back to her friends. All she wanted to do was lay down and sleep. Her hands throbbed and her shoulders ached.

Green lights? Shouldn't they be blue? She stopped to take in her surroundings. All the rock looked the same to her. Faint scuffs and breathing meant someone was ahead of her. Maybe they knew the way out.

She shuffled forward, squinting in the dim glow.

There was no mistaking Fagin's shape. He crouched and took something from his pocket. The vial! He put it against the wall, and his voice rose and fell in a chant. He wasn't listening to the trolls!

"No!" Frostine dropped the canteen and dashed forward. "You mustn't!"

He kept chanting. Grimacing face stretching his scars, Fagin seized her arms and propelled her past him, into a dark tunnel. She tripped over an unseen rock, and fell. Just as she climbed to her feet, the vial exploded in a bright flash. Blinded, Frostine staggered, arms out, trying to feel her way to safety.

The ground shook, sending her reeling. Her sore ribs crashed into a protruding rock. Pain paralyzed her, and she fell into a motionless heap.

"Get out! Cave in!" Distant voices reached her.

Her body wouldn't move.

The wall in front of her split with a crack of thunder. A narrow line forked like lightning and widened. Rocks tumbled from the ceiling. Frostine choked on thick dust, each cough sending agony through her.

Another thunderous boom, and the wall in front of her exploded, sending an avalanche of gems and stone toward her.

As darkness claimed her again, her last thought was she was tired of getting knocked unconscious.

CHAPTER SIX

PRINCE DASHIELL

DASHIELL'S EYES FLEW open as he bolted upright at his desk, heart pounding. The shrieking wards stabbed spikes of pain into his skull as he shook off grogginess and swiped at a paper stuck to his cheek.

Falling asleep at his desk in the middle of the day. What passed for day around here, anyway. What was wrong with him?

That alarm meant a cave-in at the mine. Perfect. Just what he needed. This was what he got for letting Fagin rush things. The man had saved his life, and Dashiell felt he owed the man a second chance, but he should've left the trolls in charge of the mine.

He sprinted through the manor house, down the stairs, and out the door. The mine was only a few hundred yards away and he sprinted through the trees, bursting into the mine entrance. Dust billowed in the air. Fagin bellowed ineffectual orders. A troll argued with him. Dashiell came to a stop next to them.

"What happened?"

The red-faced, bespectacled troll jabbed a finger at Fagin. "He used that ruddy magic instead of listening to us, that's what happened! After we told him not to!"

The trolls were ostensibly under Fagin's command, but the man was meant to listen to them!

"Did everyone get out?" Dashiell counted seven trolls and a group of men, but the dust in the air made it hard to be sure how many as everyone rushed around. He forced his arms to remain at his sides so he didn't punch Fagin. He'd tried to do the man a favor after battling Alphas for so long, but this was stupidity. No one wanted to be here, but risking lives was not acceptable.

Fagin hemmed and hawed.

"Did they?" Dashiell bellowed.

"All but one." A frowning troll tipped his bearded chin deeper into the mine, where six of them worked to clear the entrance, passing rocks down their line.

Swearing, Dashiell pulled the collar of his shirt over the lower half of his face and ran into the mine. Only one tunnel was blocked.

"Is there danger of another cave in?"

The bespectacled troll shook her head. "No. The mine is stable now that magic isn't forcing rock to its will."

Dashiell eyed the tons of stone. This could set them back days. Weeks.

He scooped up an abandoned pickaxe, scrambled to the top of the rock pile, and levered rocks out of the way. Workers joined him and they opened enough of a hole for him to squirm through.

This was his responsibility. He'd led men into battle and each loss of life haunted him. He'd thought running the mine would help the kingdom, and he wouldn't have to worry about men dying under his command.

"Hello? Can you hear me?" Only the echo of himself answered. He slithered through the rest of the way. "I need light."

The glowing stones that normally lit the tunnels had gone out. Fagin and his shortcut.

A frowning troll slid through the opening, lit a pair of torches, and handed one to Dashiell.

He gasped as light reflected off a diamond as long as he was tall. As he stepped closer, the torch illuminated the vision of an angel. The huge, sparkling gem lay atop the form of an unmoving woman, making her seem like she was inside it and had been mined from the wall. Ruby red lips. Onyx hair. Pale skin. He was sure her eyes would be the color of precious stones, too. He stared at her, willing her to wake. She remained still. Her chest didn't move.

Dashiell dragged himself farther into the chamber, seeing now the diamond was propped on a rock over her, the underside hollow.

"Bring rope." He dropped to his knees and maneuvered an arm under the diamond to touch her. His fingertips touched soft, cool skin.

The trolls followed him, bringing ropes, pulleys, and their tools.

"There's enough diamonds here to make the world rich." The tallest troll stared around the chamber, eyes round.

"Why is she in the mine?" Dashiell demanded, knotting the rope into a harness around the giant diamond. The woman didn't have the muscles or calloused hands of someone accustomed to this sort of work. In fact, the hand he could see was red and blistered. She wore an odd assortment of ill-fitting clothing that probably belonged to the trolls.

Frowning troll aimed an accusing finger in Dashiell's face. "She chose to work with us instead of whoring after *Fagin* bought her."

"What?" Nausea rolled through him. "Whoring? *Bought* her?"

"From slavers."

"Oh, for — " What else had Fagin been up to? He'd crossed a line. Slavery was outlawed, punishable by death. There wasn't any protection from this. "Bring the gurney. Hold the diamond up. I'll pull her out," he ordered in a normal tone, then lowered his voice to address the frowning troll. "Tell the guard to arrest Fagin and lock him up. Quietly."

The normally scowling troll grinned. "Gladly."

He ran off while the other trolls made quick work of rigging the ropes, and pulled, lifting the diamond a few feet into the air.

Dashiell tugged the woman free as gently as he could, freeing her from her sparkling prison. She lost none of her beauty outside of her diamond prison. He knelt next to her. Rage filled him at the sight of her injuries.

Her torn lip. One side of her face bruised, her eye blackened and swollen. A ring of bruises marred her neck. Those were the result of a beating, not the cave in. If Fagin had touched her, Dashiell would murder the man himself.

She wasn't breathing. He pressed his head to her chest. A faint, slow heartbeat was music to his ears. Sealing his lips over hers, he blew air into her lungs — once, twice, three times. Four.

The woman breathed in a convulsive breath. Eyes the color of the darkest blue sapphires opened and met his for an eternal moment before they fluttered closed. Her chest rose and fell as she breathed on her own. He ran his hands over her gently, but even unconscious, she winced when he touched her ribs.

Dashiell hovered over her while the trolls set to work clearing a way out. They didn't have a hospital — just a clinic where typical mining injuries were treated. It was no place for her. He'd take her to the manor.

An eternity later, a troll shoved a fold-able legless cot into the chamber. Dashiell lifted the woman onto the gurney. They strapped her down, maneuvered her through the gap, and rushed her to the manor.

With his angel settled in his bed, a possessive streak ten miles wide had opened in him, and he wasn't sure he could let anyone else touch her.

"Can we do anything for Frostine?"

Frostine. Why hadn't he asked for her name before? Maybe because angels didn't need names.

The seven trolls stood in a line, worry radiating from all of them. They were her friends, and had helped Frostine before she'd become his. And she *was* his now. "She'll need a hot bath and food when she wakes. Make sure Fagin has been arrested, along with anyone you know worked with him. We also need to get that diamond to the Enchanted City."

"We'll take care of everything." The trolls burst into activity.

He retrieved a jar from the bathroom and sat next to Frostine. The magical ointment was a gift from Charming when Dashiell went to war. He'd used it sparingly over the years, and hoped it still worked. He unscrewed the lid, dipped a finger into the medicine, and dabbed at her injured lip. The magic glittered, and the cut healed.

Relieved, he smeared the ointment over her black eye and the bruises covering her throat. Her hands received a slathering, healing her blisters. He remembered her ribs. Better to be sure he hadn't missed any injuries. Stripping her bare, he covered every inch of her in the ointment, until Frostine practically glowed under the healing spell and the jar was empty.

Her body reacted to his touch. Goosebumps spread over her skin. She arched into his hands. Her tension eased, muscles relaxing wherever his fingers and her body met.

Dashiell imagined all the ways he could add color to her. Flushes as she orgasmed. Lines of punishment as she took his whip and cane. The desire to see her pale nipples the same shade as her ruby red lips made his cock harden. See her pink pussy a darker shade from the hard pounding he ached to give her.

Tearing himself away, he dressed her in one of his shirts. Having temptation covered helped, and seeing her in his clothing satisfied his possessiveness somewhat.

The tallest troll returned, toying with the end of her braid. "We've got her a hot bath ready."

He didn't want to let her out of his sight, but surrendered her to the women for now. Frostine would no doubt appreciate being clean.

But he'd breathed life into her. She was his when she woke.

CHAPTER SEVEN

FROSTINE

FROSTINE AWOKE PAIN free this time, but when she opened her eyes, hallucinations were still happening.

The bedroom reminded her of her house — a place that had once been rich, but allowed to fall into disuse. Faded tapestries. Cracked paint. No personal decorative additions. The only thing that didn't seem to belong was a mirror on the wall. Its golden frame gleamed.

A dark-haired man sat in a chair next to the bed where she lay under a mountain of soft bedding. High cheekbones and tawny skin. And a... presence about him.

She'd never met him before, but he drew her in without trying. He exuded dominance, even unconscious, and her body, awash in unfamiliar sensations, wanted him to command her.

Who was he, and what was this strange hold he had on her? Her body ached and her skin tingled as she imagined him touching her. Like she was familiar with how he could make her feel even though there was no way she could know.

Frostine returned her gaze to the man. He was big — hardly seeming to fit into the chair. Wide shoulders. Strong hands. Thick thighs. He would tower over her.

He stirred and opened his dark brown eyes. When his sleepy gaze caught her eyes, she felt herself sinking into their depths. "Welcome back, Frostine."

"Who are you?"

His eyes widened. "You don't recognize me?"

Should she? She studied his handsome face. "No. I'm sorry. But I'm still a bit confused..."

"Don't be sorry." He gave her a brilliant grin. "I'm Dashiell. This is my house. You were in an accident. Do you remember that?"

Flashes played in her mind. "Yes. Fagin used magic after the trolls told him not to. Everything blew up."

"That's about it."

Frostine touched the back of her head and ribs. She'd had at least those injuries.

Dashiell cupped her face. His big hand felt rough and commanding against her skin. He leaned so close his warm breath brushed over her cheek as he studied her eyes. "Do you have any pain?"

Not the kind that he meant. But there was an ache building between her thighs. Something about him pulled at something in her. A new part of her awakened just by being around this man. Her breathing quickened, and a needy sound escaped her throat, but what exactly she needed, she didn't know.

Moving slowly, Dashiell lifted her chin. Gentle lips pressed against hers with sweet insistence, coaxing her to respond. She'd been kissed before, but not like this. And he was a stranger. Did he think she was a whore, too?

His tongue parted her lips. Nervousness fled. Senses reeling, she gave in, tentatively touching her tongue to his, tasting him. He made a rumbling sound of approval.

Dashiell's hand gripped the nape of her neck, tilting her head as he deepened their kiss from sweet to possessive intensity.

Frostine reached for him, running her hands over his chest. He caught her wrists, pinning her hands down. She'd been called a prostitute and whore for days, and now the one man she wanted held her off.

"I definitely want to have you, Frostine. But you need to understand I demand total submission, and all of you. You'll have no one else, and do what I say, when I say, without question. The only word you will speak is my name. Do you understand?"

Her mouth opened. Was that a test? She nodded. Dashiell gave her a smile that made her feel like a mouse trapped by a cat. He slid the soft material of his shirt over her head.

"Lift your hands and hold on to the bars of the headboard." She did. The motion lifted her breasts and his eyes latched onto the sight. Her nipples hardened under his attention.

"Offer yourself to me. Part your legs."

Her heart pounded. Could she do what he said? She drew her knees up and inched them apart.

"Farther, Little One. Lay your knees flat."

She obeyed in one quick motion before she could doubt herself.

His eyes darkened as he ran his gaze up her body so slowly and heavy it was like a caress. "Stay just like that. If you move your hands I will bind your wrists."

Frostine sucked in a breath.

"Oh, maybe you'd like that?"

She would. The idea sent a hot yearning through her.

"I'll tie you up another time." Dashiell ran a thumb over her lips. "Gag and blindfold you." His eyes landed between her legs. "I will have you at my mercy. But tonight I want you to obey just because I tell you to, not because you can't disobey."

Frostine nodded again. Despite what he said he wanted from her, this man wasn't acting like a beast, and she ached for him. She yearned for his mouth between her thighs, and almost told him, until she remembered she wasn't allowed to speak.

A dark smile that made her tummy flip-flop spread across his handsome face.

She'd never wanted a man inside her as badly as this one.

His hands gripped her thighs, and his eyes held hers as he jerked her toward him. She gasped as he moved between her legs. Her heart drummed against her ribs.

Dashiell smiled at her, and her eyes remained riveted on him as he bent toward her. Helpless to do anything else, she watched his head between her thighs. When his tongue licked her clit, bolts of lightning raced over her skin. Her hands gripped the edge of the headboard as he parted her with his fingers and thrust his tongue inside her. Her body became boneless, and she fell back against the pillow.

Grasping her rear, he lifted it in his palms and pulled her closer as he feasted eagerly on her. The sensation of his tongue, his hands, and the scrape of his teeth against her flesh had her panting for air as her hips rose and fell with the rhythm he set.

She couldn't breathe. Couldn't think. She needed... needed him to.... He took one hand away from her backside to rub her clit as his tongue delved into her. That was what she needed! Her back arched off the bed as a cry erupted from her.

Frostine kept waiting for the waves of pleasure to crest, but they surged through every nerve ending. When they finally eased, she collapsed onto the bed and gazed at the ceiling as she tried to get her bearings. She'd never experienced anything like that before, and craved more. Frostine somehow restrained herself from touching him when he rose over her. However, the mindless impulse vanished when she saw the ravenous look in his eyes, tormented and starved. It was almost painful as he undid his pants and pulled them down his hips. He tugged his shirt off to reveal his rock-hard pecs, chiseled abs, and the V of his hips pointing toward his thick erection.

What are you doing? You don't know him! Part of her was ready to leap off the bed and run screaming. The wilder part of her embraced this idea of submission, and clamored with need.

Unable to stop herself, she caressed her breasts and stomach while she admired his exquisite physique. Years of training and battle had honed this man into perfection. Her thighs parted further in anticipation of him between them. This man was hers, at least for the night. His gaze latched onto her hand and followed its movements.

"Did I say to move your hands?" The huskiness of his voice caused her to shiver. He caught her hand when she went to dip it between her legs.

"I'm the only one who will be inside you, owning you."

No one owned her. But she couldn't deny she wanted him to try. But he just watched her.

"Dashiell, I need —"

A sharp smack to her inner thigh startled her into silence.

"This isn't about what you want right now, but the pleasure I take in your body."

"But —"

He smacked her other thigh, then stroked her in a soothing motion.

Right. His rules. But she was so wet. An unbearable tension building inside her. She replaced her hands over her head.

Two thick fingers pushed inside her, twisting and flexing, sliding in and out. She was so close. She just needed a little bit more.

"Do you wish to come for me, Little One?"

She nodded hard, getting another dangerous smile.

His curled fingers stroked inside her relentlessly as his tongue worked her clit. She came with a cry wrenched from her throat.

Frostine floated back into her body, only to feel him building her up yet again. Sweat broke out over her body as pleasure rose again. She tossed her head. The wet sounds her body made excited her. But it was too much sensation now, bordering on pain.

First he denied her pleasure, then he offered her too much. She bent her knees and dug her heels into the bed to push away.

Dashiell chuckled into her pussy, holding her in place with a heavy arm across her hips. "I thought you wanted to come."

She almost argued, but caught herself. She was so sensitive now another smack might break her.

CHAPTER EIGHT

PRINCE DASHIELL

FROSTINE WAS READY for him. Her swollen sex clutched at his fingers, eager for something that would give her more satisfaction.

He prowled up her body, stopping at her breasts to bite and suck her nipples into taut little red buds.

She writhed and bowed her back, but his delicious submissive kept her hands over her head and didn't speak. She was so responsive. He might be able to make her come just from nipple play.

Dashiell slid his cock up and down her slick sex and poised the head of his erection at her opening. She'd barely been able to take his fingers at first. She would be so tight.

"Eyes on me."

Her blue eyes, almost black from her dilated pupils, opened and fixed on him.

He breached her in a slow but inevitable claiming, making her feel every inch of him.

A low moan that tightened his balls escaped her red, kiss-swollen lips, but she kept her eyes on him. She gasped as her body kept taking him. Her channel was so tight.

"Lift your knees high, Little One. Spread your sweet thighs and take all of me."

Her knees slid along his body from his thighs to his ribs. Her hips tilted at the perfect angle for deeper penetration as she let her legs fall open.

He kept his inexorable thrust pushing into her as she opened to him until he was inside her, balls deep.

"Good girl " he murmured, holding still to savor the first thrust. The moment he entered her, he knew something was different. No, he'd known something was different while he watched her sleep, and again when he feasted on her. The connection between them. The way she responded. She could be the one meant for him and Charming.

Her skin was like silk beneath his hand as he ran his fingers down her sides.

She's mine.

He pulled out of her and slid back in. When she groaned, he collared her throat and lifted her head with one hand, wanting to replace any bad memories with good ones.

Dashiell kissed her, tasting her. He kissed her ear and then her cheek as he inhaled her scent of winter and evergreen. He ran his hands over the front of her and cupped one of her breasts. Her soft flesh filled his hand as he gave her nipple a tug, testing her response. She moaned, and when he did it again, a little harder, she wiggled her hips. As he moved in and out of her, she arched and cried out.

Her fingers clawed at the headboard as an even more intense orgasm rocked her body. She arched and collapsed onto the bed, trying to catch her breath. He didn't pause as he continued his relentless possession of her body.

And it was a possession. He clasped her wrists and leaned over her as he pinned them to the bed in his bigger hand, needing her to feel his ownership of her as a tangible thing. He couldn't wait anymore. Braced on one arm, he reached between them to toy with her clit. She mewled as his thumb circled that bundle of nerves, still overly sensitive from when he'd coaxed orgasms from her. But he had to feel her coming on his cock again.

He might be developing an addiction to forcing her body to come when he wanted.

Her head tilted back, her mouth opening in a red 'o'. Her back arched and her inner muscles squeezed him in a rhythmic massage the entire length of his dick.

Perfect.

Dashiell admired her exquisite body as she moved against him. He couldn't get enough of watching her reactions while he moved inside her, taking her in deep strokes.

Her nails dug into his back as he rode her fast and hard. She'd moved her hands, but he let the transgression go, enjoying the slight bite of her nails in his flesh. He'd punish her later. As his control snapped, he shifted his arms to drape her legs over his shoulders and let himself go. Pulling out almost all the way, he slammed himself into her. Her eyes widened.

He pulled out again, and thrust in. He rode her hard, snapping his hips, driving grunts and gasps from her.

Dashiell could lose himself in her. Teach her to love everything he did to her, and how to use her body to pleasure him. He pulled back and gave her another slow thrust. She was still tight, her channel resistant and clenching at the same time.

His cock pulsed as he came in a rush and almost collapsed onto her. They lay in a tangled heap as their breathing returned to normal and she nestled against him. He brushed her hair back, wanting to see her eyes, but she'd fallen asleep. When he stroked her cheek she smiled and pressed her face into his palm.

CHAPTER NINE

FROSTINE

FROSTINE WOKE FROM her doze, head pillowed on a muscled chest. Free to touch Dashiell now, she indulged. His muscles jumped as she trailed her fingers over small scars and smooth, tawny skin. He played with strands of her hair as she snuggled against him.

"How did you come to be here, Little One?"

She bit her lip, fingers frozen on his chest. How much could she tell him?

"I just want to take care of you. The rock trolls told me what they knew, but I need to know the rest so I can put a stop to the slavers."

A warm sensation bloomed in her chest and expanded through her.

"My mother left a trust for me, but I don't know how to access it. My stepmother tried to take it all, but until I turn twenty-one, she can't touch most of it. Only my allowance. She had me arrested in the Enchanted City, and the guards sold me to slavers, who brought me here. But it wasn't only me. There were other women too. When they came through the portal, I was fighting with the slavers, and the other prisoners ran into the forest."

"I'll send some men to look for them. It's not safe for anyone to be alone in the Dark or Foreboding Forests. What is your stepmother's name?"

"Prudence Collymoore. She wanted to be queen. When she had me arrested, she said it was my fault she didn't become queen. I don't know what she's talking about. She hates me."

"How many days ago were you arrested?"

"Two or three. Maybe. I can't tell if another day started since it's dark all the time."

"When do you turn twenty-one?"

"In a week."

"And what happens to the trust if something happens to you before you turn twenty-one?"

Frostine shrugged. "I don't know. Do you think she's trying to get rid of me so she can take all the money?"

He kissed her head. "Don't worry. I'm going to keep you safe. She won't harm you here."

She'd only just met him, but she trusted him. As she let herself drift off again, loved and protected, something in her soul cracked, flooding her with more unfamiliar warmth.

TUESDAY, DECEMBER 17

CHAPTER TEN

PRINCE DASHIELL

DASHIELL WATCHED FROSTINE sleep as she lay curled against him. It was early, and he'd already awakened her twice to bury himself inside her slick tightness again. Her sweet body and submissive nature took all of him every time.

He was close to falling in love with her. She had to be the one. But telling her might frighten her. Better to introduce her to Charming first and see what happened.

In addition to his dominance, she brought out a protective streak he never suspected existed inside him. He couldn't get her mistreatment at the hands of her stepmother out of his mind.

He slipped from her embrace to make his way down the hall to his office. It was early, but Charming never checked the time when he called. Dashiell refused to feel bad about possibly waking him.

"How is Frostine?" The frowning troll blocked the hallway. It appeared Frostine brought out protectiveness in others as well.

"She's fine. Sleeping. She'll be fully recovered in the morning. What happened with the arrests?"

"Fagin and three more men are sealed in the mine. We'll make sure they don't get away."

"Good. Of the miners who are left, pick a few you can trust, and search the woods. Frostine said there were more prisoners with her, but they escaped into the woods. If you find them, bring them here. We'll offer them refuge until we figure out what else to do."

"I'll see to it. The diamond has been secured. It's ready for transport."

"Perfect. Thank you."

The smiling frowny troll ran off.

Dashiell entered his office, ignored his piled high desk, and faced the mirror. "Enchanted mirror, have some pity, and find Prince Charming in the city."

A face wavered in the glass. The man's black eyes glowered from beneath thick brows. His hair and beard were so dark they looked blue rather than black. His lips curved into a smirk. Or a sneer. It was hard to tell with him. "You at least put some effort into it." The face faded, but returned. "Nothing to say you couldn't put a little more into it."

An image of Charming's bedroom replaced the man's face. Thankfully, most of his sprawled body was covered by his sheets. Black hair rumpled, he scowled as he sat up. "Dashing, do you have any idea what time it is?"

Dashiell grinned. "Oh, is it bedtime?"

"Ha, ha, Dashing. What do you want?"

"I'm calling in my favor, Charming."

That got his brother's attention and he sat up, interested. "What do you need?"

"Have you heard of a woman called Prudence Collymoore at court?"

Charming tilted his head to the side as he ran through his mental catalog of court ladies. "Older woman? Kind of a shrew?"

Dashiell laughed. "That sounds right. She has a stepdaughter she's been taking advantage of. I want a stop put to it."

"Okay." Charming yawned. "Do you know anything else about her?"

"Apparently she thinks she should have been queen, and that it's Frostine's fault that didn't happen."

"Why the interest in this Frostine?" Charming squinted at the mirror and waggled his eyebrows. "Do you have a woman at the mine?"

"Yes." Dashiell rubbed his jaw. "That's another thing we need to talk about. Apparently the city guards are selling female prisoners in the Enchanted City to slavers here in the Dark and Foreboding Forests."

"What?" Charming roared. "It's a death sentence to traffick people."

"Frostine came here through a portal from a dungeon the city guards kept her in. Her arrest was trumped up and she'd been beaten. There were other women who escaped, too. I've got some men looking into it here. You need to see what you can find out there."

"I will." Charming rubbed his jaw. "We were just boys when my father became king, but I think I remember something scandalous about the coronation." He rumpled his hair, making it spiky. "I'll see what we can do. You should come into the city and bring the girl. There may be documents to sign or some testimony she needs to give. Plus there's the party tomorrow night. We're expected."

"We'll come with the shipment from the mine today." His brother should be happy with the huge diamond that fell on Frostine.

"Come to the town house. Don't go to the palace. We'll go together."

"All right. See you in a few hours."

Now for the second item of business.

Dashiell sat on the side of the bed and stroked Frostine's pale cheek with the backs of his fingers. "Wake, Little One." Her dark lashes fluttered, then her sapphire eyes stared sleepily up at him as she stretched languidly as any cat.

"I've laid out some clothes for you." He kissed her forehead. "Get dressed. We're going to the city."

He hated the fear that came into her eyes. She clutched his hand between hers, pressing his palm to her chest. "Do we have to? Please. Can't I just stay here with you?"

"Your place is with me. Don't worry about that. But your stepmother has robbed you of enough. She needs to pay for what she's done, and we need to save whatever is left."

"My stepmother has powerful friends at court, and attorneys. They won't believe me over her."

Dashiell smiled. "I've contacted my brother. He's going to help you."

Her brow furrowed. "Who is your brother?"

"The Prince."

Frostine gasped. "Prince Charles of the Enchanted City? That's who my stepmother wanted to meet when she offered me to those men who had me arrested."

He nodded. "Yes, Little One. The only man with more power in the city is the king. Your stepmother doesn't know anyone with more connections or power. Everyone will listen to you."

CHAPTER ELEVEN

PRINCE CHARLES

CHARLIE DRESSED IN a borrowed guard uniform and pulled the helmet on. With the face plate lowered, no one would recognize him. Without Dashing here to create a diversion, a disguise was the only option to move freely around the palace. Courtiers were always laying in wait everywhere and at all times of the day and night.

He left his room and strode through the corridors toward the library. No one would ever expect to find him there. Even he didn't expect to find himself there, but it was the quickest, and least obvious, way to find out what he needed to know.

At the entrance he eyed the rows and rows of bookcases. How did anyone ever find anything in this place? There were just shelves and shelves of books, scrolls, and parchments. He wandered through the aisles, picking up random items, scanning them, and replacing them.

"Might I be of assistance?" The words were a question, but the querulous voice, mixed with some authority, sounded annoyed and condescending. A gnarled hand adjusted the spine of the book Charlie had replaced haphazardly so it lined up precisely to the edge of the shelf and its mates.

Charlie lifted his face plate and gusted out a sigh of relief he never imagined he'd feel for a librarian. Well, not for a male librarian, anyway. "Yes, please." He faced the owner of that disapproving voice.

The old man was a foot shorter than him, and a quarter of the bulk. Blond hair going to gray created a halo around his face. In one arm, he carried a stack of books so high he could hardly see over it. His slightly rheumy eyes widened. "Your Highness." He threw himself into a low bow.

Catching his arm, Charlie stopped the frail man before the weight of his books toppled him. "No need for that. I'm in disguise. Don't give me away."

"Um, er. Yes. Of course, Your, um...."

"Call me Charlie. Or my friends call me Charming." Okay, only Dashing called him that.

The librarian's bushy gray eyebrows shot up. His mouth opened and closed but no sound came out.

Charlie swept the books out of the man's arms and held them out of reach. That jolted the librarian into motion. He wrung his hands and reached for the tomes.

"I'll help you put these where they go if you tell me what I should call you. Lord Librarian? Master of Books? Seems like everyone is Lord of Something or Master of That Other Thing." He winked. "But we're friends. Right? And I promise I won't touch anything else in here if you tell me what I want to know."

The man's shoulders relaxed. "Atticus."

"All right, friend Atticus. Let's get these put back so we can move on to my project."

With the library restored to proper order, Atticus led Charlie to an office and cleared off a chair, taking his own seat behind a massive wooden desk piled high with reading materials. The strict rules of orderliness in the library did not continue into his office.

"I appreciate your help. Those high shelves are hard for me to reach as I get older. What can I do for you?"

Over the hour they'd worked together, Atticus had become positively chatty. Charlie sat but leaned forward, elbows on knees. "What do you know about Prudence Collymoore?"

Atticus, relaxed now that Charlie wasn't touching anything, tapped his finger on his chin. "Collymoore. Collymoore. Wait here." He rose to his feet and entered the stacks, returning with a thick book that he thumped on the desk. Flipping through the pages, he ran his finger down a column of densely packed, tiny letters.

"Aha. Here it is. Prudence Collymoore is the daughter of Mary and William Collymoore. Her father was given the title of Baronet for valor in battle by a previous king. Prudence married Duke Coille. She has no children, and is widowed. That's all the information we have on the family so far."

Nothing about the girl Dashing was so concerned about. Interesting.

"Duke Coille was the man who stepped aside so my father became king?"

Atticus wheezed like his lungs no longer worked. His skin took on an unhealthy shade of red and his mouth opened and closed like a caught fish.

Charlie wanted to laugh, but worried the man might die of a stroke or maybe swallowing his tongue. Was that possible? What should he do? Pound his back? Get him water? A potion?

Fortunately, the librarian recovered on his own, but didn't spout the information needed.

"Don't worry. I'm just looking for information. I'm not out to upset the monarchy."

"Er, well." Atticus pulled at his collar. "I seem to remember a bit of a to-do. Something about a prior deal affecting the succession."

"Yes. That's what I need to know about."

"But your father... Don't you know the story?"

Charlie shook his head. "It's one of those things that's Not Talked About."

"I see. As I remember, Duke Coille was next in line, but signed a contract to give up what he valued to keep what he loved."

What did that mean? "A contract with who?"

"That I don't have a record of. But you could talk to the librarian who worked here at the time. He retired a few years ago, but lives nearby."

CHAPTER TWELVE

FROSTINE

FROSTINE WAS GOING to explode if she didn't get some relief. There was hardly any point to being dressed — Dashiell had his hands on her skin almost as soon as they'd entered the carriage. She shook with the need he'd been building in her. He hadn't stopped touching her for the entire duration of their journey. It had seemed to take hours and mere minutes at the same time.

When the carriage finally stopped, she trembled with need. Dashiell scooped her into his arms and carried her into a townhouse. He swept past the butler who opened the door, a maid in a black and white uniform on the stairs, and into a bedroom, where he kicked the door closed and set her on the end of the biggest bed she'd ever seen.

She laughed as he pounced on her and her clothes disappeared with yanks and ripping sounds as she playfully tried to dodge his hands. Naked, she lay pinned under him, his black leather clothes warm and soft against her bare skin.

"I think I've spent more time naked than I have clothed around you."

"I'm not seeing the problem." Dashiell closed his lips over a nipple and sucked until the bud formed an achy peak. His fingers slid up her thigh to her sex and delved inside.

She squirmed. He'd teased her over and over, but left her unsatisfied for hours. "Please. Not again."

"I'm going to bind your wrists while you wait for me."

Her eyes widened and her stomach fluttered. If that's what it took to stop this prolonged torture, she was happy to be tied up. She held her wrists out.

"Kneel here for me." Dashiell patted the edge of the bed. When she moved into position, he wrapped silk around her wrists and stretched her arms to the wooden posts. He drew a third strip of silk across her skin, then tied it over her eyes.

Her breath hitched. Being bound was one thing. Bound and without sight in a strange place was another.

"You aren't gagged. Little One. Do you have anything you want to say?"

Did she want to tell him to stop? No. She wanted to see what would happen. He wouldn't hurt her.

"No. I'm all right."

Dashiell pressed a kiss to her forehead. "I love how you trust me. Wait right here, Little One. I'll get you some food. When I come back, I'm going to reward you."

Frostine breathed out a sigh of relief that he swallowed as his mouth took hers in a slow, sweet kiss. His footsteps crossed the room and the door closed.

While she waited, she rubbed her thighs together and pulled at her restraints. Dashiell had tied them too well.

A warm exhale across her ear made her jump.

"Dashiell?" Surely he wouldn't leave her naked and bound where other people could find her.

"Shhhh." He sounded like Dashiell. Fingers stroked across her cheek, down her neck, and along her arm. All things Dashiell had done before, yet the touches felt different now. His hands felt smoother, less calloused, but still commanded her body to respond.

While the physical touch felt different, the connection felt the same. But if the hands were different, was this a new man? Could she feel the same sort of bond with two men?

What did that make her? Unfaithful? Was she actually a whore?

He'd shushed her, but the silence was unnerving. "Please."

Frostine stopped with the single word, afraid of what words would come next. Stop? She didn't want that. Don't stop? She shouldn't want that.

She needed relief. Something inside her. A way to release some of the tension coiled low and deep within her. Footsteps came down the hallway. Whoever was touching her backed away as the door opened.

"Charming." Dashiell's voice held a growl as he crossed the room. His familiar touch untied the blindfold, restoring her sight. He draped a blanket over her. "Are you all right, Little One?"

Frostine nodded, relieved Dashiell didn't seem angry with her. She glanced between the two men exchanging murderous glares. They could have been twins.

"Dashing." Charming sounded hurt. "You didn't tell me you found *her*."

"I wasn't sure. I thought so, but I wanted her to meet you first, although I hadn't planned to introduce the two of you like this."

Charming held up his hands. "I don't begrudge you finding her first. You've had to change so much to cater to my needs. It seems fitting you should find the perfect woman for us."

"Dashiell..." Was this a test? He hadn't told her about the rules. Had he left her tied up here so this other man could find her?

"Yes, Little One?"

"I'm not a whore."

"That's not what we think, Frostine." Dashiell tipped her chin up with a gentle, but firm finger. "Little One, this is my brother, Prince Charles."

She gasped, closed her eyes, and pulled on her restraints. The Prince! And she was meeting him like this! He'd think she was like her stepmother! "Your Highness —"

"Call me Charming, please. And he's Dashing. You are a dream come true, Princess. I am delighted to meet you."

"You are?"

"I want us to be very well acquainted."

Frostine's gaze flew to Dashing. He smiled. "He won't hurt you."

Charming touched her cheek again, and she looked back at him. "We've been searching for a woman both of us can love. You're the only one we're both drawn to. We want you to be with both of us."

"How does that work?" She leaned toward Dashing. The Prince was equally as handsome, but he was the Prince!

"Whatever happens between us is not wrong and only between us. You can choose one or both of us, Little One. Not only for this, but in our life. There is no wrong decision here."

Was that possible?

"Do I frighten you, Princess?"

"No." She probably should be at least nervous, but she wasn't. His desire for her made him seem more like Dashing rather than the Prince.

"One of us can have you while the other one watches. Would you like that, Princess? Knowing you're being watched?"

She found her gaze drifting to Dashing again. "You...you would like that?"

"You'll find there is very little you can do that we won't like, Little One." Dashing untied the silk from her wrists and settled himself against the headboard, drawing her to him. With her back to his front as she reclined, he watched Charming explore every part of her without hesitation or shame. It was as if he could not get enough of her.

After an empty life, with no attention or love, she had two men. She'd just met them, but their adoration was clear. More warm sensations expanded from her heart.

Charming kissed her mouth until it felt swollen, and she whimpered as he ran his tongue down the line of her throat to her breasts. As he palmed one, he suckled the other nipple, pulling gently until it was red and erect.

Frostine had never felt so excited by someone playing with her breasts, and when he moved to her stomach, she fought a moan of disappointment. She smelled her arousal. Instead of nuzzling her between the legs, he skirted that neediness, working his way down her hips and thighs.

Dashing cupped her breast and pinched her nipple. She opened her mouth to cry out, but his hand on her throat stilled her, his thumb caressed her throat, comforting and frightening at the same time.

Charming worked over every inch of her, kissing and caressing. When he stroked the backs of her knees, she nearly yelped, but with firm pressure, he adjusted the sensation from ticklish to sensuous.

"Please," she whimpered.

"You can take it." He shifted up, pressing her knees apart. Despite her eagerness, Frostine couldn't help shutting her eyes tightly. There was something intimate about being observed by Dashing while she twisted with pleasure at Charming's touch.

But Dashing liked watching — the evidence of his enjoyment pressed into her back, although he made no move to do anything about it.

Frostine moaned as Charming ran a gentle hand along her inner thigh, stopping just short of the heat between her legs. She gasped when one finger pressed inside her with a sweet pressure that made her hips buck.

She looked into Charming's brown eyes, darkened with lust. Dashing's hands palmed her breasts while Charming's finger pushed in and out between her legs.

He eased a second inside her, gathered some wetness, and slickened her clit. He slid the pads of his fingers against her sensitive skin. The heat collecting low in her belly unraveled as every muscle in her body tightened.

Her body shook with desire, hands clenched into tight fists and her knees pressed hard into the bed as she arched. Her eyes flew open as the pleasure peaked, and she looked straight up into Charming's eyes as she gave herself up to the bliss.

She arched up into his hand, her entire body trembling.

CHAPTER THIRTEEN

PRINCE CHARLES

CHARLIE LEANED IN SO their faces were inches apart. "Say my name," he said intently. "I want to hear my name on your lips, Princess."

He wasn't used to being second best. He was the Prince! Frostine was far too aware of Dashing.

"Charming," Frostine murmured obediently, her voice husky from her orgasm.

He growled deep in his throat. In a single motion, he pulled his hand away and came to rest on top of her. His body pressed between her splayed thighs, and his hard cock moved against her slippery skin.

"Tell me you want me,"

"Charming, I want you. I want you..." Frostine moaned, and ran her nails down his back. She did it harder than he expected. The bite of pain made him arch, and he groaned.

"I can't resist you." Charming entered her with a single motion. He moved over her, determined to possess her. At first he kept his thrusts slow and steady, but with every moment, he grew more frantic, less controlled.

"I want you," she kept saying, "I want you. I want you, Charming."

Sweat beaded his brow when she moved her hips insistently, impaling herself, begging for it harder and faster. He gave her everything, holding nothing back as he powered into her over and over.

The sound of their flesh slapping filled the room along with moans of pleasure. His balls tightened as his release climbed. He gritted his teeth, trying to wait for her.

"Touch yourself, Princess. I need you to come now."

Frostine didn't hesitate. Her hand grazed his cock as it plunged in and out of her wet sex. She trembled as she worked her nub.

She was perfect.

Charlie went deep, twisting his hips to hit her just right.

When she shuddered through her orgasm, clenching down on his cock, he thrust himself into her one last time, filling her with the essence of his release. His climax made him feel light-headed as it blazed through his body.

His deep groan echoed in his ears, and his full weight slumped down over her. For a moment, he was simply still, then he tilted his head to one side, kissing her sweetly. He stayed within her, connected, enjoying the moment of closeness.

WEDNESDAY, DECEMBER 18

CHAPTER FOURTEEN

FROSTINE

FROSTINE LAY BETWEEN her lovers. Utter contentment left her limp in their embraces. It was more than a physical satisfaction. This must be what it felt like to be... loved.

The crack Dashing had started, widened with the addition of Charming's feelings for her.

The barrier created around her heart, and keeping her numb since her father died, dissolved. Heat made her feel languid and liquid. Bit by bit, the warmth spread through her, leaving her with the sense of being wrapped in a soft blanket.

Happiness made her feel light. Like she could soar and fly with the swan and ducklings from the park. She imagined rising above the bed and floating to bask in these feelings.

Physical touch vanished.

Frostine opened her eyes.

She hovered above her body. In a panic, she thrashed, trying to sink and go back into herself. A tug pulled her toward the window. Chill breezes tickled her intangible body and recalled distant memories of freedom. If she went out, she'd never get back to her body. If that breeze carried her away, it was forever.

She whirled and peered into the mirror. A fog hovered over the bed, where her body lay between Dashing and Charming.

What was happening? She'd just found love and somehow she was changing into what? A ghost? Had she died like her mother and father? What had she done in her life to deserve hatred, and now, just when she found love, she was dead?

Dashing! Charming! Help me!

Her fog self had no mouth, and so no voice. Her princes couldn't hear her. Drops of water formed in the fog and dripped onto the men below.

Dashing and Charming stirred. The deep slumber of the sated was slow to release its grip on her princes, but they bolted upright when they realized something was wrong. She could do nothing but watch in horror as her princes tried to wake her.

Dashing held her hand and cupped her cheek. "She's so cold."

"What's happening?" Charming pulled the covers back. "Frostine?"

Frostine.

That was her name.

The wind trying to take her away grew more aggressive, swirling harder and faster, pulling her toward the window. *No! I want to stay!* Even without her body, she could stay with her princes.

They looked up at the ceiling like they could feel her.

"Frostine." Dashiell reached for her. "Come back to us, Little One."

"Princess, don't leave."

Her bodiless self drifted toward the window. Frostine reached for her princes. A disembodied hand formed out of the mist she'd become. Dashing and Charming shivered as she touched them. She curled her fingers, trying to hold on, but her hand slipped through them.

Even so, some remnant of what she had been didn't like seeing their despair over what she had become. They touched the empty thing that had been her, anguished voices murmuring and shouting words she didn't understand.

The pull from outside the window increased, and she couldn't remember why she didn't want to go. She could do one thing for the men before she went.

She put her disembodied hand on the still figure between the men. The shell that used to hold her. Already it felt less and less like her, but she could touch it.

Color seeped from the body. The skin turned translucent. Eyes paled from sapphire to white. Red lips faded to pink, then a blue tint. Black hair grayed and faded.

A coating of ice started at the toes and flowed up the body until it was encased, and looked like an ice carving that sparkled inside. There. Now the men would always have what she had been.

She reached out with ghostly fingers, but they were useless. Her fingertips slid over the ceiling as her spirit was pulled out the window, swept away on the wind, and carried into the sky.

CHAPTER FIFTEEN

PRINCE DASHIELL

"WHAT THE HELL HAPPENED? People don't turn to ice!" Dashiell rushed around the room pulling on clothes. "Maybe Frostine was under a curse. Something that spiteful stepmother bitch did to steal her inheritance. It's her birthday soon. We have to help her."

He'd felt her spirit float out the window, taking vital parts of him with her.

"A witch. Maybe the one who —"

"I know where we have to go." Charming stared at the ice statue that had been Frostine. "But you're not going to like it."

"Where?" Dashiell threw Charming's princely pants at his head. "I'll go anywhere for her."

"The Foreboding Forest. We must find the King of Winter."

"What?" Dashiell paused, one arm halfway in his sleeve. Of course it was the Foreboding Forest. At least Frostine wouldn't melt there. "The King of Winter?" Well, that explained the ice, but not the why or how.

Charming nodded and pulled on his pants. "Ice. We need ice. The diamond is still in the cart. It's hollow. We can fill it with ice and take Frostine with us. There's no time to waste."

Here was something he could do. Dashiell pulled on his boots and headed for the door. "Ice!" he bellowed, clattering down the stairs. He raced into the kitchen. "We need ice!"

Several kitchen workers jumped to attention. "How much ice, Your Highness?"

One good thing about being a doppelganger to a prince was no one ever asked useless questions when they thought he was Charming. "All of it. Get it from the neighbors, too. Every piece of ice you can find quickly. I'll be back for it."

People rushed off to get ice for no reason other than the prince wanted ice.

Back upstairs, Charming was dressed and had fashioned a platform wrapped in sheets that he was sliding under Frostine's ice statue body. "If we just lift her, she might break. I'm not sure what will happen then."

As if their woman turning to ice wasn't bad enough, now they had to worry about her melting and chipping.

"You better be right about this, Charming."

CHAPTER SIXTEEN

FROSTINE

OUTSIDE THE WINDOW, a breeze spun her through the city as it whirled her higher. She struggled, desperate to return to the men. Why did she want them when she had the world? Chill wind swept her into a bank of clouds. Cold froze her in place and something of herself vanished, taking her cares with it.

Free of what held her back, Frostine soared into the sky. She left behind the disagreeable buildings and entered a forest. The branches, leaves, and pine needles brushed against her and she laughed.

She flew toward the ground, leaving a swath of pure, crystalline white snow behind her. Reaching out, she sent more snowflakes to decorate the landscape as she flew east. That way was home.

Winds carried her into a forest of darkness, then farther, into winter. Snow lay on the ground and icicles hung from black tree branches and cavern eaves. She spun in a slow circle, then faster and faster, sending new snow around her in a blizzard.

She'd been here before. This was her home!

Snegurochka.

That voice. That word.

Snowflake.

Snegurochka

Joy filled her. She hadn't heard that voice in so long.

Papa?

Out of the whirling snow, a white-bearded man dressed in white furs emerged.

"It's time to return home, Snegurochka."

She became wintry wind, and she followed him home.

CHAPTER SEVENTEEN

PRINCE CHARLES

DASHIELL TRIED TO URGE the horses to greater speed, but it was no use. Charlie knew how he felt, since he was trying to make the wagon fly by sheer will. The spelled wagon was as fast as transportation could go, but it felt like the trip was lasting an eternity.

"After we talked, I went to the library and checked into the events surrounding the coronation, and why my father was chosen. I tracked down an old man who told me that Duke Collies and his wife, Frostine's parents, loved one another beyond life, but they were never able to conceive a child. Then, one day they had a daughter, a little girl, but never spoke about where she came from. It just became the accepted thing, because their daughter was only kind to everyone, and eventually no one cared where she'd come from."

Dashing gave him a sidelong look as they passed from the Outer Forest into the Dark Forest. "So they adopted her?"

"Right." Charlie glanced backward to where Frostine lay covered in ice. Well, it wasn't Frostine anymore. But it was all they had left of her. "When the king died and it was time for the Duke to be coronated, he refused and gave up his title. He showed a contract with the King of Winter in which he'd given up what he valued, riches and fortune, to have what he loved, and the crown went to my father."

"But what deal?"

"I don't know." Charlie shrugged. "But given that the Duke's daughter just appeared one day, and the deal was with the King of Winter, and now Frostine is ice, she must be that girl. The King of Winter must know what is happening to her."

Unfortunately, the King of Winter had a reputation for giving visitors icy receptions.

CHAPTER EIGHTEEN

PRINCE DASHIELL

SO, THE KING OF WINTER gave the Duke a daughter. How did that relate to what happened to Frostine now? The horses galloped along the main road. People, carts, and heavily loaded wagons scattered before them. At the border with the Outer Forest, the track narrowed and grew rougher. He was torn between going faster and worry he would damage Frostine's... body.

No. He couldn't think she was dead.

Eternal night engulfed them as they crossed into the Dark Forest, and finally, they entered the Foreboding Forest, always caught in winter no matter the time of year. Gnarled, bare branches reached toward them and gray clouds pressed down on them from above, bringing icy winds.

In their haste to leave, they'd not brought winter clothes. He shivered. Despite the hostile atmosphere, a little relief trickled through him. In this weather, Frostine wouldn't melt.

Dashiell brought the horses to a stop. "Okay, well, we're here. We won't be able to take the wagon any farther. No paved roads here." Well, not anymore. The wolves preferred their territory wild. "We'll have to carry Frostine from this point." And hope the wolves left them alone.

"You know the area better than me. How do we find the King of Winter?" Charming jumped from the seat and strode to the back of the wagon.

In all his campaigns, Dashiell hadn't come across the King of Winter. "The heart of this forest is where the Alphas have their fortress. He won't be there. And west is the sea, so that way is out. I think we go north, toward the mountains."

There'd been no reason to go to the mountains when he fought here during the wars. He wove ropes together, forming a harness they slid around the diamond. Walking side by side, Frostine suspended between them, he and Charming entered the woods.

The earth turned from frozen dirt, to snow that drifted up to their knees, to ice that threatened to twist their ankles.

A flurry of snowflakes whirled toward them, congregating around Frostine in her ice-filled diamond. The little storm intensified, growing denser, and blocking the sculpture from sight.

"Frostine? Is that you?" Maybe he was imagining it, as desperate as he was to get her back, but he thought he could feel her touch and see a glimpse of her face in the mist. It wasn't her though. Or, at least not all of her.

He sighed. "Let's go."

They trekked toward the mountains. His feet turned numb inside his boots and his fingers felt brittle as the black branches around them. Like they might snap off. Cold air stabbed into his lungs with every breath. Even when he'd fought in the Foreboding Forest, it had never felt so cold. They had to be going the right way.

Charming slogged next to him, breath coming in great heaves that he expelled in foggy plumes. He was struggling with the unaccustomed physical exertions, but didn't complain.

Hours later, they broke out of the tree line. The base of the mountains loomed in front of them — a nearly vertical gray wall. A palace of ice and stone perched on an outcropping a couple hundred feet overhead.

The home of the King of Winter.

No trail led up the mountain, but the uneven terrain provided plenty of hand and footholds. They'd have to climb.

Dashiell re-rigged the ropes so the diamond holding Frostine hung sideways between himself and Charming. "Ready?"

Charming tilted his head back to eye the way up to the palace. "Let's go."

"Stay near me. Don't follow the blue lights. The Will-o-the-wisps will lead you astray."

CHAPTER NINETEEN

FROSTINE

WOLVES RACED BENEATH her, raising their voices to howl at the full moon. A great snowy owl's soft feathers joined her as they flew. She swooped low, skimming the frozen surface of a pond. Spreading out as far as she could, she let the wind carry her, drifting in a contented doze. It felt nice to take whatever form she wanted.

A discordant clatter of noise disturbed the quiet. Two men with horses that pulled a wagon rushed through the trees.

They stopped and carried something heavy into the woods.

Feeling a pull toward them, Frostine flew after the pair. They could be twins, but they were just humans. Why was she drawn to them? Watching them made her simple joy lessen. She didn't like that, but couldn't look away. They made her feel like she'd forgotten something important.

Did she know them? Maybe they knew who she was.

She swirled around the sparkling rock they carried. There was something that called to her about the sculpture that hung between them.

CHAPTER TWENTY

PRINCE CHARLES

CHARLIE'S MUSCLES SCREAMED and long-frozen fingers threatened to lose their grip on the rocks he clung to. He'd lost track of time as his world narrowed to the few inches of rock wall in front of him.

The temptation to look up or down and gauge their progress was hard to resist, but he forced himself to focus on the next hand or foothold. He reached for the next handhold, found a new foothold, and pushed himself up.

Dashing moved smoothly as he kept to Charming's pace. He was much better at this outdoors stuff.

They climbed steadily. Charming fell into a trance as his body went through the motions.

The rock he braced his foot on shifted, and he slipped. He dug his fingers into the hand holds. The stone underfoot crumbled, leaving him dangling.

"Charming!" Dashing watched, unable to move to help.

Charlie lost his grip, fingers slipping off, leaving him scrabbling, pulled further off balance as the rope harness yanked him to one side.

A rope, covered in snow and frost, snapped, and the diamond swung, spilling ice in a shower toward the ground. The uneven weight snapped another rope. The diamond, containing Frostine, fell.

"No!" His heart plummeted. He wanted to look away. Didn't want to see Frostine, even an ice sculpture of her, smashed against the unforgiving ground below. But his eyes riveted to the diamond and its precious cargo.

His clumsiness had killed her.

Wind gusted, lifting the diamond holding Frostine and carrying her overhead toward the palace. Relief wiped away exhaustion. Full of new energy, and without the weight linking them and threatening to drag them off the wall, he and Dashing raced upward.

In minutes, they pulled themselves onto the ledge next to the palace, rolled onto their backs, and panted. The palace loomed over them. Carved from ice in shades of blue, silver, and white, curving onion domes topped high towers.

Dashing recovered first, and jumped to his feet, pulling and prodding Charlie. "Let's go."

He ordered his weary body to move and followed Dashing.

The doors to the palace stood open, and they ventured inside. Everything was ice. Dark blue columns lined the sides of the corridor. The floor was white and translucent. Gray clouds floated above them, hiding the ceiling. Ice torches burned with the same eerie lights that appeared in the forest.

Their boot steps echoed as they walked down the hallway. Double doors opened, admitting them into a throne room. The ice here had color, like it had been painted, and depicted winter-themed mosaics.

Blue ice formed a carpet that led the way to the front, where a white-bearded man wearing fur-lined robes and a crown of ice sat on his crystalline throne. In front of him, lay the diamond that held the ice sculpture of Frostine.

"Approach."

Charlie exchanged a glance with Dashing and they walked along the blue path. It was strange being the one approaching the throne rather than watching someone walk toward him. He didn't like being the petitioner.

They came to a stop in front of the seemingly only person in the palace. What was the protocol? He'd seen more than one meeting go horribly wrong when insult was taken where none was intended.

The ruddy-cheeked man fixed his blue eyes on them — eyes the same sapphire shade as Frostine's. Had the king given the duke *his* daughter? Why would he do that?

"I am the King of Winter. Who are you and why are you here?"

Charlie bowed. "I am Prince Charles of the Enchanted City. This is my brother, General Dashiell." His brother hated the title, but Charlie felt the need to make this king understand his visitors were important men of means. Well, in title, anyway.

"Why have you come to my home?"

"Frostine." He couldn't help a longing glance toward the statue that had been his lover. "She turned to ice. We thought you would know how to..." *Fix her* seemed like the wrong thing to say. The King of Winter probably didn't think there was anything wrong with Frostine as she existed at the moment

"To what?"

Charlie floundered for words. Dashing jumped in. "To return her to us."

"I am the King of Winter. What do you suppose that makes my daughter?"

"She's a Princess." Charlie bit back the *Mine* he wanted to shout. "I knew it."

Dashing elbowed him.

"Why would I return my daughter, a Princess of Winter, to you, when she has only just come back to me?"

Dashing shifted from foot to foot. "I think she cares for us, and we care for her."

"You met Snegurochka's human form. She is an elemental winter spirit, never meant to be confined to a human body. The woman you knew as Frostine no longer exists. She's left that life behind."

"She can't have forgotten everything." Charlie spoke the words for himself as much as the king.

"You mean, you think she'll remember you? Perhaps." The king drummed his fingers on the throne's arm. "But you shouldn't get your hopes up. The longer she is elemental rather than human, the more wild she will become."

Then they had to get her back quickly.

CHAPTER TWENTY ONE

PRINCE DASHIELL

"HOW DID FROSTINE... Snegurochka, come to be human in the first place?" Dashiell had so many questions. If they could make Frostine human again, he could make her remember. He knew it.

Two seats of ice appeared out of a pair of small blizzards, and the King of Winter waved his visitors to sit.

The King glanced at the ice statue, and sighed. "My Snegurochka was always curious. She wondered about the humans we saw when we went for walks in new snow. We came across the duke and his wife. They had built a daughter of snow since they couldn't have one of their own, and we listened as they imagined the life they would have together.

"My daughter begged for a chance to live among the people she was so curious about, and I agreed, provided they treasured her more than riches and taught her about love over her life with them."

"That's what the contract was for." Charming looked too big for his ice chair as tension practically vibrated through him.

The King inclined his head. "A human affectation. The Duke insisted on it."

"That's all we want to do — love her." Dashiell wanted to touch the cold statute but curled his hands into fists.

"My daughter has no reason to cherish most of her time among your kind, though, does she?"

The words were like a knife to his gut. Next to him, Charming gasped. Frostine's stepmother had treated her poorly, and caused Frostine to be sold into slavery.

"Instead of learning love, my daughter learned hate and indifference. Her ice heart grew colder, instead of gradually warming, yet she ignored my calls to come home. She remained too human to hear me. When she discovered love with the two of you, instead of thawing over time, her ice heart melted. She cannot live as a human without a heart."

"Her stepmother did that to her." Charming's leg bounced up and down. "We already have a plan to deal with her."

The King of Winter frowned. "That's not all she has done. The Duke's second wife poisoned the first to take her place, and when he refused the crown, she poisoned him."

"What?" Charming shot to his feet. "There was never any indication of that."

"Well, why would there be? Humans often kill one another without anyone the wiser. And my daughter was left in the hands of a murderer."

Charming drew himself up. "I can assure you, if there is any way to prove Prudence Collymoore has committed murder, I will see to it she pays for her crimes."

"What difference does it make now? My daughter is safe." The King offered an icy smile and held up one hand. A blizzard blew around his fingers. "The Duke and his wife loved my daughter. The least I could do was prevent them from rotting. You will find their bodies are perfectly preserved, as is the evidence of the poison that killed them."

They were getting off track. "That happened before we met her. We can make sure she is cherished every day. Her stepmother will never harm anyone again." Dashiell stepped forward, hands held out in entreaty. "Please, can't you make her another heart?"

"We can teach her about love," Charming added.

"I could make her another ice heart, but I fear the same thing will happen. Her feelings are too strong. If she melts again, she will be only spirit."

Dashiell leapt to his feet. "Give her my heart. It belongs to her already." If she remained dead, he didn't need it anymore.

"No!" Charming jumped up. "Use the diamond."

"No. The kingdom will go bankrupt."

Charming leveled a glare at him. "If he takes your heart, you'll die, Dashing. You've been with me my whole life. I can't lose both of you." He faced the King of Winter. "Last time you let your daughter take a human form, two people gave riches to prove they valued love more. Take the diamond. It's all I have to offer."

The King of Winter steepled his fingers and studied them. "You both love my daughter. That's all I ever wanted for her. I will use the diamond to contain her new heart. However, it was my daughter's choice to take a human form before. It will be the same this time. If she wants to be with you and live in your world, that is her decision."

CHAPTER TWENTY TWO

FROSTINE

SHE HOVERED NEAR THE ceiling as gray clouds and watched the men with Papa. The statue she'd made for them lay in the shiny case. They'd brought it here, but almost dropped it. It would have smashed if she hadn't caught it. She longed to fly again, but something about these men kept her in the palace. They were talking and talking, but their words were just noise.

How far could she spread her mist? Enough to cover the whole room? The entire forest? She stretched out. A spider lived high in one corner. When her mist touched the web, little icicles hung from the crystal lines of the web.

She could make more lines. A web as big as the room! She could make the strings through the palace. A thread of ice spun from her fog, attaching to the ceiling on both sides. She made another line to cross it, then a big circle to go in the middle.

Snegurochka.

She turned from the web. *Yes, Papa?*

He stood next to his big chair and smiled up at her. *Did you hear what we were talking about?*

She spun in a big whirl all the way around the room. *No. I like to hear their voices, but I don't understand their words. I was trying to see how big I can be, and now I'm making a web.*

You're remembering all the things you can do. Papa sent snow from his fingers and touched her web, making thicker threads and adding shades of blue and silver. *These men want to take you to the human world, Snegurochka. Do you want to go?*

With them?

He nodded.

You want me to leave you, Papa?

Of course not. You aren't a child anymore. If you return to the human world again, this time you will remember who you are and what you can do. You'll know me and be able to take your elemental form. Your home will always be open to you.

She looked down at the men. They had moved from their chairs to kneel next to the statue. *Should I go?*

I want you to be happy. If they love you, and you love them, be with them.

I like being winter. She glanced back at her unfinished web. *I love the wind, and the trees, and making snow. Do I love the men, Papa?*

I believe so, or you wouldn't be here watching them. Listen to what they say.

Their words are just noise, Papa.

Listen with your heart and decide what you hear.

What about my web?

It will wait for you.

She swirled down from the ceiling and around the men as they talked to their statue. They looked sad, and she didn't like that. Was the part of her that didn't like their sadness her heart? She concentrated on listening, and their voices turned from noise to words.

"We'll move to the Foreboding Forest so you can be near your father."

"We'll make sure you know love every day."

A part of her felt like she flew through the forest without moving.

"Come back to us, Little One."

"You'll have to be treated like a Princess now."

The more they spoke, the more she wished she could speak in return. The feeling she was supposed to be someone else intensified.

I want to go with them, Papa.

Then I will make a new heart for you. His magic lifted the statue, letting the men hold it up between them.

She imagined she felt their hands on her, and she shivered.

The shiny rock the men had carried rose into the air surrounded by a whirlwind of winter magic.

An icicle formed in a blizzard and struck the gem like a hammer, shattering it into millions of tiny sparkles. They whirled in the air together with a magnificent storm of ice and snow in blues, whites, and silvers of Papa's magic.

The mixture expanded to encompass the two men, the statue, and her mist. An avalanche of emotions rushed through her. Hope. Pleasure. Happiness.

Love.

Everything spun together, shrinking into itself and coalescing into a heart of diamond dust, love, and Papa's magic.

He gathered the beautiful heart into his hands, and walked toward the statue.

"It's time, Snegurochka."

She flowed around the heart, the men, and the statue. As her mist settled into the ice sculpture, Papa pressed the heart into her chest.

The men leaned forward. Twin sensations pressed to her cheeks. Warmth spread through her, flowing from where lips met her skin to the rest of her, all the way to her toes. The sensation wound back on itself, all the tendrils coiling to join in her chest. Love bloomed there, making her diamond heart beat.

"The ice is gone."

"She's warm."

Frostine blinked up into two pairs of dark eyes.

"Little One!" Dashing pulled her close and kissed her.

"Princess." Charming turned her in their embrace and kissed her.

"My princes." They helped her to her feet. "You saved me."

"Snegurochka."

"Papa!" She turned to him and staggered, trying to remember walking instead of flying.

Winds caught her and set her down in front of her father. She threw herself into his arms. "Thank you for my new heart, Papa."

"You are welcome. Since you will remember who you are this time, I expect to see you often."

"Yes, Papa." Frostine kissed his pink cheek.

Frostine sat between Charming and Dashing on the bench of their wagon as they raced through the Foreboding Forest. "What are we going to do now? Will we go to the mine and see the rock trolls?"

Dashing shook his head. "Not yet. We can fix up the manor house and live there, but first, we have to end this situation with your stepmother."

"What will happen to her?"

"She'll be arrested for fraud and murder."

Murder. Sadness made her sway. Her human parents, the ones who had loved her unconditionally, had been killed by Prudence.

"Will she go to the same jail as I did? She could end up here!"

"I've got something special in mind for her." Charming hugged her tighter to him. "She will never hurt you again. You're safe."

She rested her head on his shoulder. "You've given me a heart made out of the diamond that was supposed to save your kingdom. I don't need money. Can I give it to you? Do you know if I have enough?"

"Everything helps. We'll speak to my father." Charming lifted her hand and kissed her fingers. "If he accepts your offer, it will only be a loan. We'll keep the mine going and pay you back, with interest. We'll do everything right, so you're not taken advantage of anymore."

"We also have a party to attend. We'll introduce you to court tonight, and there will be no doubt about who you are or your standing."

Introduce her to the court? She'd lived hidden away so long, she wasn't sure if she was ready for that.

Dashing nudged her with his thigh. "One of us will be with you the whole time. Don't worry."

When they reached the Enchanted City, Dashing left the horses at a stable. Charming dressed in a guard's uniform, with a helmet that hid his face, and escorted her through the city to a street full of shops she'd never visited, stopping in front of one with a closed sign on the door.

"What is this place?"

"The dressmaker's. You'll need a gown for tonight, and she's the best." He banged a heavy fist on the door.

A woman with a friendly smile and a rounded figure greeted them. Her blue gown swished around her sandaled feet as she rushed Frostine into the shop.

"The ball starts in hours! Shame on you for waiting until the last minute! How am I supposed to dress her with so little time?"

Charming gave the woman a grin. "If anyone can do it, you can."

"Out with you, then. We can't have you here in the way."

Charming was shooed out, with a promise to return for her.

"Those boys didn't leave us much time, but we'll get you ready. First, a dress."

The woman took Frostine's hand and guided her up and down the aisles. Gowns in a rainbow of colors and lengths didn't appeal to her.

Then, she saw it. Discarded across a chair, lay a white dress with a lace overlay. The lace contained a snowflake pattern.

"That one." Frostine headed for it.

"Oh, that one is naught but a scrap of practice one of my girls was playing with to work with lace." The woman wrung her hands.

Frostine picked up the dress anyway and held it to her body. "This is the one."

"It's plain and not finished. Hardly more than a slip! Not suitable at all for a formal event like the ball tonight."

"Is the girl who was making this dress here?"

The woman nodded, giving in. "Natalie, please come here."

Footsteps pattered through the store, and a waifish girl with pins held in her lips and a tape measure wrapped around her slender body appeared from around the end of an aisle.

When she saw Frostine holding the dress, the girl's blue eyes went round as saucers. Her mouth dropped open with a squeak, spilling pins down her front to the floor.

With another squeak, Natalie dropped to her knees to gather them. "I'm sorry, ma'am. I shouldn't have left that out. It's just that I was sewing, then some ladies came in, then I had to fix a hem, and then — ouch!" A drop of blood bloomed on her finger and she shoved it into her mouth.

Frostine crouched to help gather pins. "Natalie, I think this dress is beautiful. I can sew a bit myself. Do you think if I helped, that we could finish this for tonight?"

"Um, yes?" Natalie chewed her lip. "My lady?"

"If we're going to work together, you should call me Frostine."

Natalie nodded so hard Frostine's neck ached. "Yes, my lady Frostine."

Frostine slipped on the half sewn dress.

Natalie transformed from a shy, indecisive mouse of a girl to a young lady confident in her abilities. "I wanted the dress to look like winter, since that's the season, and the theme of the party. The pattern in the lace reminded me of snowflakes."

Adept, nimble fingers made short work of the hemline and side seam while Frostine pinned lace across the new neckline, bodice, and sleeves.

When they were done, they stood side by side to examine their work. The dress was still more slip than ball gown, close fitting with a slim, floor-length skirt, sleeves of lace, and daringly low neckline. Snowflake lace rose from her breasts to her neck, ran down her arms, and dotted the skirt.

Natalie sighed. "It's almost like I imagined, and you look beautiful, Frostine. I pictured more sparkle, though. Maybe we should use some sequins? Do we have time?"

Frostine doubted her princes would wait much longer. "Can you keep a secret?"

"Of course." Natalie gave another head rattling nod. "The only person trusted more than a lady's hairdresser is her dressmaker."

Frostine wasn't sure about that, but let the wild, elemental part of herself out. A wintry breeze spun through the air, starting at her hem and swirling around her, all the way to her neck. The pattern in the lace became actual snowflakes, no two alike, as they sparkled in blue and silver against the white material and her skin.

Natalie gasped. "That's perfect!" She clapped her hands. "Now you're ready for the ball."

CHAPTER TWENTY THREE

PRINCE CHARLES

"SO THERE'S NO DOUBT about it?" Charlie stood at the foot of a pair of sarcophagi. As the King of Winter had promised, the Duke and his wife were perfectly preserved.

The Court Witch lowered her hands. She wore a purple hooded robe that hid her features so she could move around in anonymity when she wasn't working. "No. Your information is accurate. They were both poisoned."

"Can you track the poison back to the person who used it?"

"It's been years since they died. I can try, but it might have been too long."

"I know who did it, but I have no proof."

"Will your source testify?"

Charlie almost snorted laughter at the idea of summoning the King of Winter to testify in court. "I don't think that's practical, but we might be able to send someone to take testimony."

The witch shrugged. "In my experience, someone who has successfully poisoned people in the past may very well have poison around in case another opportunity presents itself. Poisons like this take time to prepare and require unique ingredients."

"I'll have someone search the property." He'd have to figure out a way to get Prudence out of the house. Maybe she'd like a personal invitation to the ball.

IN THE ANTECHAMBER to the ballroom, Frostine, resplendent in her snow and ice gown, stood next to Dashing in his black military dress uniform. Charlie had allowed himself to be wrangled into a white tunic and pants with too many gold buttons, embroidery, and stripes.

Eric, the Captain of the Guard, wearing a formal blue uniform, approached. He grew up at the palace with Charlie and Dashing, and could be trusted. There was still the matter of wrongfully arrested women being sold into slavery to deal with.

Charlie heaved a sigh.

The Captain bowed. "Your Highness, Prudence Collymoore has been here for an hour and the search was successful. We consulted with the Court Witch, and found the exact same poison."

"Men you trust are in place?"

Eric nodded.

"Thank you for letting me know." He stepped back to Dashing and Frostine, bending one arm for her to take. When she slid her arm through his, he led them to the announcer.

"Introduce her as Princess Frostine, daughter of the King of Winter." He paused. "And my betrothed."

Frostine stared up at him, eyes wide.

Charlie flashed her a grin. "I'd call you my wife, but we didn't have time to get married this afternoon."

Speechless, she turned to Dashing.

He kissed her forehead. "We don't need to shock everyone that you're mine, too, and I prefer to keep out of the spotlight."

Charlie patted Frostine's hand. "You will not be hidden away anymore. Everyone will know who you are, including your hag of a stepmother."

They took their places at the top of the stairs leading into the ballroom. They waited at the top of the stairs while below them people in ball gowns and suits milled and mingled. Tables of food and drink lined one wall, glass chandeliers lit up the huge space, and an orchestra sat at the ready on a platform to the left. To the right his parents watched over the proceedings from their thrones on another platform.

The announcer stepped forward, accompanied by a blare of horns. "Prince Charles, General Dashiell, and Princess Frostine, daughter of the King of Winter, and betrothed to Prince Charles."

The crowd stood motionless for a moment, then burst into applause. His father's lips pressed into a flat line. His mother beamed at him.

One woman with an elaborate hairdo and gold ballgown with a huge skirt stared at Frostine, her expression full of hatred. She had a beauty so sharp it might slice a man to bits. Charlie caught Eric's glance, and inclined his head. The blue-uniformed guards moved through the crowd toward her.

"Prudence Collymoore," Eric boomed. "You are under arrest for fraud, embezzlement, murder, attempted murder, trafficking, and prostitution."

Frostine clutched at Charlie's arm, staring as guards surrounded Prudence, took her arms, and led the sputtering, red-faced woman out.

Charlie leaned down to whisper, "Your home is yours, as is every cent in your trust. You'll never see her again."

DASHING TWIRLED FROSTINE at the end of the song and escorted her to Charlie. As they reached him, he handed a flushed Frostine a glass of champagne. Dashing stared at the entry stairs and groaned.

Charlie turned to follow his gaze and grinned. "Well, things are going to be interesting now. We might be upstaged."

Two enormous men wearing black uniforms, and a striking woman dressed in a red gown, stood at the top of the stairs. The red-faced announcer looked like he might be having a heart attack as shocked murmurs ran through the crowd.

The dark man didn't wait for the announcer, now opening and closing his mouth with no sound, and escorted the woman in the red dress down the stairs. The larger man patted the herald on the back, which didn't help anything, and followed the other two.

"Who are they?" Frostine asked.

"The men are Alphas." Charlie grinned. "I have no idea how they got an invitation."

Dashing snorted. "Lupin and Mojek don't usually require an invitation."

Frostine sipped from her drink. "Who's that woman with them?"

"I've never seen her before."

"She's beautiful."

The trio paraded through the ballroom like they had every right to be present. The dark man led the golden-haired woman in red onto the dance floor while the bigger man stood to the side. He gave an unfriendly looking woman a resigned stare as she headed toward him like an arrow.

Charlie led Frostine onto the dance floor, taking a position next to the interlopers as the music started. They moved alongside the other couple.

"So, are you the forward scouts?" he asked in an overly loud whisper. "Are we about to be overrun?"

"Clearly you're the Charming one." The blonde grinned impudently. "I'm Petra. This is Lupin, and our friend there is Mojek. We don't mean to cause trouble. We heard about the ball and wanted to show we can be civilized."

Petra elbowed Lupin, who lost his scowl. "We want to negotiate peace and bring the wars to an end."

If the realm didn't have to maintain an army, the mine kept up its output, and with the loan of Frostine's money, the kingdom might claw back from the brink of ruin. He had to tell his father. Charlie gave Dashing a look, and he started across the dance floor.

"I'm Frostine, and you're right. This is Charming, and the man approaching is Dashing."

"It's lovely to meet you, Frostine." Petra smiled. "Your dress is amazing."

"It's lovely to meet you. Your dress is beautiful, too."

"I've got to get to the dais. The greetings are about to start." Charlie sighed. "I'll be back as soon as I can. While I'm up there, I'll mention that you want to talk peace to my father."

Lupin nodded.

Charlie turned Frostine over to Dashing and made his way to his parents. The news that the Alphas wanted to talk peace should soothe any ire from his father about the surprise announcement of his betrothal.

CHAPTER TWENTY FOUR

FROSTINE

AFTER THE SONG ENDED, Petra linked her arm with Frostine's and led her away from the men. "They'll posture at each other for a while. In the meantime, you and I can talk, then we'll tell them what they've agreed to."

"But..." Petra seemed nice, but Lupin was an Alpha. He radiated menace and her winter magic strummed under her skin.

Understanding the concern, Petra put a hand on Frostine's arm. "Don't worry. Lupin and Mojek are Alphas, but they want to end the fighting. They won't start any trouble."

She glanced over her shoulder and smiled at the Alpha, who shifted from trading glares with Dashing to bestow a look of such adoring heat on Petra it was amazing the woman didn't burst into flames.

Petra nudged Frostine with a playful elbow. "Smile at your prince before our men punch each other in the nose and mess up their handsome faces."

Frostine laughed, and as Dashing met her eyes, she gave him a wink and smiled at him, receiving an adoring look of her own.

"There. That should keep them calm for a few minutes." Petra led the way to a table offering a variety of desserts and sampled a cookie. "Not bad, but the Dowager Dove's are better." She filled a plate and held it out, offering to share. "So, how did you meet your princes?"

It felt like she'd known Charming and Dashing forever, but it had only been a couple of days. So much had happened. "My stepmother had me arrested and the guards sold me to slavers in the Foreboding Forest."

Petra went rigid. "They sold you to slavers?"

Frostine stared at her. She didn't seem like the same woman. This version of her seemed more like an Alpha.

"I'm sorry." Petra softened her expression. "I didn't mean to get so intense. One of the things we're trying to stop is kidnappings and trafficking in the Foreboding Forest. By the time I find the women, they've already been taken. This is the first time I've had a clue where they're coming from."

"You find them in the forest?"

"Yes. Some friends and I patrol the forests looking for troublemakers. Did you see any faces? Would you recognize the slavers?"

"No. They wore hooded robes. But they took me to a man named Fagin. Dashing had him arrested. He might know more about who the slavers are."

"What about the guards at the prison?"

"It was dark most of the time. I couldn't see their faces very well, but they all seemed to be in on it. None of them seemed surprised or tried to stop what was happening."

Petra smiled. "The prison is a place to start. Thank you."

"There were other women with me. They ran into the forest the night I was taken to the mine." Frostine gripped Petra's arm. "They need help."

"Where were you when they ran into the woods?"

"I don't know. I'd never been to the Foreboding Forest before, and they knocked me out before I was taken to the mine." She wasn't a scared girl anymore. "I can probably find where the portal opened." She might not have remembered the forest before, but her magic knew the forest now.

"That's great. And as long as we're in the city, we can talk to the guards at the jail. Lupin loves to have *friendly* chats. Unless you've already spoken to them."

Frostine shook her head. "I've almost died twice in the last few days. We've been busy."

"Will you tell me where the prison is?" Petra set the empty dessert plate on the table. "Parties like this aren't really my thing. I can think of something else I'd rather be doing."

"You're going to fight?"

Petra nodded and picked up a glass of champagne from a passing waiter. "I could use a good workout. You don't have to come with me. I —"

"Oh, I'm coming, too." Frostine touched a finger to the flute glass Petra held. Ice froze the champagne left in the bottom and sent frost over the glass. "I can take care of myself, and want to see the guards pay for what they did."

Petra's green eyes sparkled. "Let's go knock some heads."

CHAPTER TWENTY FIVE

PRINCE DASHIELL

"WHAT ARE YOU DOING here?" After receiving the wink from Frostine, Dashiell relaxed a bit. But only a bit.

Lupin's eyes flashed gold. How close was he to losing it? It wasn't smart to challenge an Alpha, but Dashiell couldn't help it. He'd been on the front line too often.

The Alpha shifted his gaze to the woman in red. Petra smiled at him, and the man's body relaxed. He loved her. Dashiell could relate. He only had eyes for Frostine. She laughed at something Petra said, her whole face lighting up.

"I see you know how it feels." Lupin's voice, more conciliatory than Dashiell expected, brought his attention back to the matter at hand.

"I'd do anything for her." The words were out before Dashiell thought better of speaking them.

"Even talk to me?" Lupin sipped his drink. "I recently took over as Alpha of the Foreboding Forest. The wolves won't be fighting wars anymore."

Dashiell wasn't sure he believed that. It was true there had been fewer skirmishes lately, but there were factions within the wolves. Just because a new Alpha said not to fight didn't mean all the wolves would listen, and Alphas had a way of dying quickly.

The peace could die when Lupin did.

The Alpha narrowed his eyes at something. Dashiell swiveled to see Mojek running out the doors to the garden.

"Now what?" Lupin growled, eyes on someone else.

Dashiell spun in the other direction. Arm in arm, Frostine and Petra slunk toward another door.

"What are they up to?"

"Trouble." Lupin set his glass down and stalked after them.

Exchanging a glance with Charming, Dashiell followed the Alpha.

CHAPTER TWENTY SIX

PRINCE CHARLES

CHARLIE HATED THE POMP and protocol these events entailed. At least his place atop the dais gave him a good vantage point.

Petra and Frostine stood away from Dashing and Lupin. They had the look of women up to something.

"Frostine is lovely." His mother offered him her cheek. "When do we get to meet her?"

He placed a kiss on her cheek and shook hands with his father. "Tomorrow, when all this is over. I needed to remove some obstacles to ensure her safety."

"Meaning Prudence?" Father sounded relieved.

"She was one. Now that Frostine's life is safe, and her fortune is secure, she has offered to loan it to the realm. Between that, and peace with the Alphas, we may avoid bankruptcy."

His parents let their royal masks drop for a second to show surprise. "You are full of news tonight, my son."

The receiving line began, and Charlie shook hand after hand.

A woman with an unfriendly face matched glares with Mojek as she marched in his direction. The giant murmured, and moved to head her off.

They argued in quiet tones, the woman pointing to a young woman standing with an older, owlish man. Apparently, his parents weren't the only ones intending to make matches tonight. The woman gestured, and the owlish man pulled the girl toward them. He practically shoved her at Mojek.

A second woman, who may well have been the girl's twin, entered the hall from a door to the outside garden. She scanned the crowd, her expression falling when she spotted Mojek with the other girl. She doubled over, arms wrapped around her middle. Mojek pushed the first woman away and sprinted toward the second as she turned and fled outside.

What was that all about?

Lupin and Dashing looked ready to murder each other until Petra and Frostine calmed them from across the room.

At a break in the receiving line, Charlie turned to his father. "Lupin and Mojek are here to talk peace. Will you meet with them?"

"We will hear what they have to say tomorrow morning."

Petra and Frostine, arm in arm, headed for an exit. Those two were definitely up to something. He shook hands with the noble in front of him, paying him as little attention as possible. Catching Dashing's eye, Charlie inclined his head ever so slightly in the direction of the skulking women. Frostine would have to be punished for trying to abandon them. Where did she think she was going?

Dashing and Lupin moved through the crowd. The women quickened their steps and vanished out a door.

Charlie turned to his father, an excuse ready.

"Go." The king waved a hand. "I know better than to try and keep you. Do try to be around for peace talks with those Alphas. Dashiell, too."

"Yes, Father." He left the dais and joined Dashing and Lupin as they followed Petra and Frostine through the city.

They paused as the women came to a stop. Frostine lifted her hands, sending whirlwinds of magic off in several directions.

While they waited, Petra lifted her skirt and removed a bundle of red cloth folded several times. She shook it out, revealing a red hooded cape that she draped over her shoulders. An axe and a hatchet appeared in her hands as she drew them from under her cloak.

Dashiell gaped. "Is that..."

"Yes." Lupin smirked.

"The Crimson Hood is a..." Charlie gave a low whistle.

The Alpha crossed his arms, never taking his eyes from the woman in red. "Yes."

Frostine's winds returned, and she led Petra farther into the city.

"There's an old jail this way." Charlie wished he was wearing any other color than bright white with far too many gold trimmings. "Shouldn't be in use anymore."

"Sounds like a good place to sell prisoners from."

Unfortunately, it did.

The women walked up to the door and knocked. Petra hid off to one side.

"That's the plan? Knock?" Charlie laughed. "I have to give her credit for keeping it simple."

A blue-uniformed guard opened the door. "What do you want?"

Charlie squinted at the man. "Their uniforms are nearly identical, but not exactly like an actual guard."

Frostine announced, "We're with the office of prisons here to do a surprise inspection."

"Office of prisons?" The man sneered. "You have no authority here." He ran his eyes up and down Frostine's body. "I remember you. Maybe you liked it here. You want to be arrested again?"

Petra stepped to Frostine's side.

"It's the Crimson Hood!"

"You have the right to remain silent." Petra hit the man in the face with the butt of her hatchet. He collapsed soundlessly.

The door opened and a contingent entered the street to surround the pair of women.

Dashing started forward only to be stopped by Lupin's hand on his shoulder. "I don't know about Frostine, but Petra gets annoyed when I interrupt her fun. And I really want her to be happy when she's wearing dresses like that one under her cloak."

"There are eight of them against Petra and Frostine!"

"I know." Lupin leaned back against the wall and crossed his arms, stretching the fabric of his sleeves. "Frostine will be lucky to get one or two. Petra doesn't share very well."

Charming gave the Alpha a disbelieving look. "You just let her run into danger?"

Lupin snorted. "Nobody *lets* Petra do anything. And if she's working with Frostine, Petra trusts her to handle herself."

CHAPTER TWENTY SEVEN

FROSTINE

FROSTINE SUCKED IN a breath as guards surrounded her and Petra. The urge to run nearly sent her flying into a blizzard. Before she could, Petra whooped, and burst into action. She threw a punch that knocked one guard out, then spun, lashing out with a kick to a second man's midsection, followed by her other leg, catching the doubled over man in the head as she whirled.

A third man reached for Frostine. Raising a hand to her lips, she blew across her palm, sending a flurry of snowflakes into his face.

With a triumphant laugh, Petra leapt into the air, tucked into a flip, and landed behind two men. She kicked a sword out of one's grasp and used the butts of her weapons to strike their heads.

Another guard grabbed Frostine's arm, but jerked away with a yelp as ice ran up his arm. She didn't know how to fight like Petra, not yet, but wouldn't be a victim again.

Petra's weapons spun and blurred as she deflected sword strikes. The sound of metal striking metal rang through the night.

Frostine created a freezing wind that blurred around the blades. With Petra's next blows, the swords shattered.

"Don't tell Lupin, but I might be in love with you."

A giggle startled Frostine as it burst out of her.

More guards ran from the building, but slipped and slid on ice that formed under their feet.

"Now what?" Frostine, hands covered in miniature blizzards, put her back against Petra's, hardly able to recognize the woman she was turning into. This sort of behavior had never occurred to her when she'd lived with Prudence.

"Now, we let the boys in on the fun." Petra jumped to dodge a strike to her leg, and kicked one of her opponents in the neck, then dropped low and whirled, sweeping her foe's feet from under him. "Lupin?" she called into the darkness. "It's your turn."

A growl came out of the darkness, so feral a sound Frostine's blood turned to ice. The Alpha's snarl had the same effect on the guards and they froze as they tried to get to their feet.

The largest wolf Frostine had ever seen emerged from shadows as inky black as his coat. The second snarl was even more terrifying, accompanied by a flash of white fangs and glowing golden eyes.

How had Dashing fought against Alphas like this one all these years?

The wolf paced forward, Dashing and Charming on either side of him. The men drew swords as the three of them rushed into the fray.

"Come on." Petra pulled on Frostine's arm. "The boys can handle this. Let's see if there's anyone who needs to be freed, or if any other guards are trying to escape."

Frostine sent her winds into the building ahead of them. "There are people below, but not on this level."

They sprinted into the jail past empty offices and barracks to a staircase. A row of lanterns stood on a shelf. Petra didn't hesitate as she grabbed one, lighting it as she hurtled down the stairs.

The woman had no fear. A reckless thrill rose in Frostine as she barreled after the red cloak into the darkness.

They moved down a dark corridor full of wooden doors, flipping open the latches, and pushing doors open. Four women emerged, but no more guards.

Frostine led the way into the bathing chamber and the cavern where the portal opened. "This is where they sent me to the Foreboding Forest. I don't feel any magic now, or the forest."

"I think it's the slavers who use it, so that makes sense." Petra sheathed her hatchet and axe on her back. "I really want to know where they're getting their spells. If I could figure that out, I think that would disrupt their trafficking more than anything."

Petra gave Frostine a speculative appraisal. "Those are handy talents you've got. We could use your help in the forests."

Frostine couldn't help a swell of pride. "Dashing and Charming said we can live in the Foreboding Forest so I can be close to my father."

"Then we'll be neighbors. I've moved into the Alpha's fortress in the forest."

"That means I can help!"

"We'll have to get you a cloak."

Frostine touched her dress and used her magic to adjust the snow and ice to create a hooded garment like Petra wore, but made hers a light blue.

"Or that works." Petra grinned.

Frostine returned her cloak to a snowy dress, and followed Petra back through the corridor, where four nervous women, hardly more than girls, huddled near the stairs.

Growls, grunts, and groans filled the air.

"It's all right, they're on our side." Petra handed the lantern to a woman and darted upstairs, but when they arrived, the fight was all but over. Blue-uniformed guards lay on the floor.

Charming, his white uniform less pristine, Dashing, looking satisfied with himself, and Lupin, gold eyes wild, dealt with the last few men on their feet.

"Ladies, you're free to go." Charming offered a courtly bow and extended an arm toward the door.

"You mean... we're not arrested anymore?" The brunette holding the lantern eyed the way to the door like it was a trap.

Charming held up his hand."I, Prince Charles, hereby absolve you for whatever crimes you were arrested for. We summoned a coach. It will drop you off wherever you like. If you need a place to stay, head to the palace and tell the guards I sent you."

The woman murmured their thanks and filed out.

CHAPTER TWENTY EIGHT

PRINCE CHARLES

AS THE WOMEN LEFT, and Charlie straightened from his courtly bow, pain ran through him, starting at his back and radiating to the rest of his body.

Frostine screamed, her anguished eyes fixed on his. No, she stared lower. He moved his eyes down and stared at the tip of a sword protruding from his chest.

Dashing roared, leapt, and swung his sword. Something fell to the floor. No. Not something. Someone. The man who had stabbed him.

The man who had *stabbed* him.

There was a sword in his chest. And the laundress would never be able to get that dark red stain out of his white tunic.

Charlie collapsed to his knees. Hands caught him and laid him on his side. Voices and words blended. He blinked and tried to focus.

"We need a doctor." That sounded like Dashing.

"There's no time." Petra.

"I've seen wounds like this before. If we pull the sword out right now, he'll die." Lupin.

Charlie tried to speak. It seemed like he should have a say in what happened to him. Or some eloquent final words. He was good with words. That's why he was Charming.

But no words came out. No breath would come in.

"I can freeze him. I mean... I know how to preserve him, but my magic can't heal him." His Frostine sounded bereft.

He'd done that to his Princess. He should have made sure the men were unarmed or unconscious.

"That can help. The blade is through his heart. If you freeze his heart, that will slow his bleeding enough for the change to take effect." Lupin again.

Frostine, in her snow and ice dress, knelt next to him, and finally he could see her. She nodded. "I'll do it."

Do what? The change? His thoughts felt sluggish. It was hard to keep up.

Winter magic flowed through him and he lost track of words. A snowstorm whirled under his skin as an icy sensation ran through his body. It was a welcome feeling and took the pain away. Frostine's magic settled in his chest, leaving him floating in a powdery cocoon.

Lupin's form blurred. The man disappeared and the huge black wolf surged forward.

Time slowed down as Charlie realized what change the Alpha intended. Lupin was going to bite him. He'd never thought about how more wolves were created.

He had no doubt he was dying. Would he rather die than become the thing he'd been at war with his whole life? One of the monsters that prowled the forests, terrifying the populace? Would the people of the Enchanted City accept a wolf for a prince? Would he still be Charming?

Charlie met Dashing's eyes. There was devastation.

Frostine wept. Her tears fell on him like snow.

He wanted more time to live. To love. They'd just found Frostine two days ago. It wasn't nearly long enough. If he wasn't already dying, the King of Winter would surely murder him for making Frostine cry.

There wasn't a choice. Not really.

Charlie tilted his head to the side and bared his neck to the wolf.

Mostly numb in Frostine's magic cocoon, there was more pressure than pain when Lupin struck fast and deep, sinking his fangs into Charlie's shoulder and holding fast.

Petra moved around behind him. "Hold him. I'll deal with the sword."

Charlie's blood burned, ruining his perfect hazy numbness, and he thrashed. Hands held him down.

"The change is starting. Let go of your magic, Frostine." Petra yanked the sword from his body.

Charlie's vision grayed and blurred. A vast emptiness in his body grew. Something warm and wet gushed down his chest and back.

Blood. They were letting all his blood out. It seemed like that should be kept inside. This time there was no pleasant floating. Darkness gave him no choice as it seized him and dragged him into an abyss.

Charlie lay still, feeling... strange. His body felt like it belonged to someone else and he was a visitor. It was bigger and smaller. Whoever this body belonged to was powerful. Strength overflowed the muscles.

"He'll wake soon. I can hear his heartbeat. It's growing stronger."

He recognized that voice. Lupin. The black wolf had bitten him because he was dying, and that's why he felt so different now.

He wasn't human —he was a *wolf*.

With that understanding, his new form made sense. Four legs. Odd, but not insurmountable. His tail thumped on the floor. That was definitely weird. He blinked and opened his eyes. Sights were keener. Two men and two women sat on the floor near him. Each of them had a bright glow that made his eyes hurt. Everything was too loud. His nose filled with too many strange scents that made him dizzy. A whine trembled in his throat. He closed his new eyes and wished he could shut his ears.

"Find what you love and block everything else out." Shockingly, Lupin didn't have the greatest bedside manner.

A female scent of snow and ice and magic intermingled with a male smell and grew stronger, freezing all else out. Possessiveness, and the urge to rend and shred the man touching the woman, filled his mind. She was his.

Ours, a distant voice insisted.

His.

Ours, the voice insisted.

Dashing. Frostine. *Ours*.

Keeping his eyes closed, Charlie followed their combined scents. Two pairs of hands touched his fur — one pair small and delicate stroked his ears, the other larger and calloused rested on his shoulder. The two people he cared about more than anything.

He opened his eyes. Frostine and Dashing were in front of him, and his world righted.

Frostine smiled through her tears. "You are the most beautiful wolf I've ever seen."

"What big teeth you have." Dashing ruined the moment. "What big eyes you have."

Charlie snarled at Dashing.

Dashing only laughed. "What big attitude you have."

Charlie rolled to his stomach and carefully stood on four feet. He hated the tentativeness of his first steps, but he didn't fall. He peered around.

"Here."

Winter magic brushed across his fur and filled his snout as Frostine created a silvery sheet of ice.

His reflection shocked him. He'd known he'd see a wolf, but not this.

On four legs, his head reached above Dashing's elbow. White fur tipped in the icy blue and silver colors of Frostine's magic covered his body. Gray eyes brightened to silver.

Frostine hugged his neck and kissed his nose. "I'm so happy you came back to us."

"I'm not going to kiss your nose, but I'm glad, too." Dashing nudged the wolf's shoulder. "Can you shift?"

How was he supposed to become human again?

Wanting it seemed to be all that was required. In moments, he crouched, naked. His body ached like he'd run for miles. Or scaled a mountain to get to the King of Winter's palace.

He cleared his throat and asked Lupin the most important question. "How come you get to keep your clothes when you change back and forth?"

Golden eyes aglow, Lupin smirked. "They're spelled to shift with me. We can get some of the same for you."

Petra held out a pile of blue uniforms. "Some of these might fit. At least long enough to return to the palace."

"Thanks." Charlie sorted through the clothing and pulled on the largest pants. "What else do I need to know about being a wolf?"

"You are not just a wolf. You're an Alpha. I can sense it."

Charlie laughed. "My father is going to love that."

"Like he wasn't bossy enough as a prince," Dashing muttered.

Lupin went on. "You're going to want space to run. Especially during the full moon. The city will likely feel too crowded. You'll need to adjust to feeling more aggression. Until you learn to control your senses, you may feel overwhelmed, even as a human."

"Yet another reason to move to the Foreboding Forest as soon as possible."

"In the meantime, what are we going to do with these men?" Dashing nudged an unconscious prisoner with a boot. "As it turns out, we happen to have a spare prison available."

Petra frowned. "Is imprisoning them here the best idea? What if the slavers come back?"

"Keeping them here is convenient for tonight." Lupin glared at the fake guards in disgust. "We work with a witch. She can get answers out of our prisoners."

"The court witch can interrogate them." Charlie snarled at conscious prisoners.

Lupin smiled, which was more frightening than his growl. "No offense to your court witch, but our witch has a more... Deft touch when it comes to interrogations. We'll contact her."

Charlie stood, arms crossed, glowering at their captives. "All right. I'll place new men here to keep up the pretense this place is still functioning. They'll alert us if anyone shows up. In the meantime, my father has agreed to meet you. We can arrange rooms in the palace. How's tomorrow morning for peace talks?"

Lupin inclined his head. "The sooner the better. We need to return to the Foreboding Forest as soon as possible."

CHAPTER TWENTY NINE

PRINCE DASHIELL

DASHIELL LAY AWAKE in Charming's huge bed in the palace. He had his own rooms, but he hadn't wanted to be separated from Charming and Frostine last night.

Charming, exhausted from his near death and multiple shifts, had fallen asleep as soon as they arrived in his room. Frostine lay tucked against his side.

He wasn't sure he could sleep again. Seeing Charming nearly die, Dashiell had felt like it was his heart the sword had pierced.

No one talked about it, but one of the reasons he'd been brought to the palace when his likeness to Charming was discovered was to die in place of the prince. To attract danger to himself and keep Charming safe.

But he'd failed. He should have noticed the man moving to pick up a sword. Made sure they were all dead or bound. Charming wasn't used to fighting. He didn't understand the dangers.

And Dashiell had been able to do nothing to save him. Lupin and Frostine had worked their magic while he'd looked on helplessly.

Now, Frostine was a winter elemental, and the Prince was an Alpha.

"Your heart is beating too loud," Charming complained. "It wasn't your fault."

"You almost died. You *would* have died."

"But I didn't. And now I'm some sort of ice wolf. I feel magic when I'm in my wolf form. I'm excited to see what I can do."

"Probably should wait until we get out of the city first."

Charming opened one silver eye. "You're no fun, Dashing. Maybe we should find a near death experience for you so you can come back as a rule breaker."

Frostine stretched and gave them a sleepy smile. "Lots of chances to break rules in the Foreboding Forest."

Dashing groaned. "Petra is a bad influence on you."

"Petra is fun," Frostine murmured. "She's going to teach me to fight."

"I think it's for the best that I'm changed now." Charming sat up and flexed his new muscles while leering at Frostine. "I wouldn't have been able to defend myself. Now I can. Lupin has offered to teach me to fight as a wolf. You can teach me to fight as a human."

The sun rose and streamed in the window.

Charming kissed Frostine and slid out of bed. "Let's get these peace talks out of the way so we can leave. I'm already feeling the need to run."

Dashing hoped he could keep up.

CHAPTER THIRTY

PRINCE CHARLES

BECOMING A WOLF, NO, an *Alpha*, had done nothing to make Charlie more patient with things like peace talks. The wolf side of him prowled under his skin, itching to leap forward and use teeth and claws to solve everything.

No wonder they fought all the time.

Forcing his attention back to the meeting, Charlie held in a sigh. Frostine and Petra were with the Queen, leaving him with Dashing, Lupin, the King, Eric, and a few advisors gathered around a conference table. Tea was served. Small talk ensued.

Things like this normally took weeks of negotiations. Charlie was not looking forward to it.

Lupin shifted in his seat. The teacup he'd been offered looked ridiculously tiny in his big hands.

Charlie picked up his teacup. Yeah, ridiculously tiny. He set it down before he crushed it. His mother liked her tea services. He might be an Alpha now, but no way was he going to be responsible for breaking up a set.

Despite Lupin's outwardly calm demeanor, Charlie's new senses informed him the Alpha's impatience with the mutterings, ditherings, and timid glares in his direction was near an end. Charlie hid a grin and waited for the fireworks.

The teacup and saucer in the Alpha's hands made the barest clink as he placed his untouched drink on the table. "Let's just state the facts, shall we?" Unlike the quiet teacup, Lupin's voice cut through every other sound in the room, plummeting the meeting into a tense silence.

"I am Alpha. The wars are over — among the wolves, and with you."

Charlie had to admire the efficiency. No concessions given or demanded. The decades-long war was just... over.

"We have a common enemy in the Foreboding Forest and in your city," Lupin went on. "Slavers who use magic to appear and disappear. Now that we aren't fighting each other, we need to unite against them."

"Slavers?" The King's heartbeat skipped and several advisors gasped. "In the Enchanted City?"

Charlie sat forward, feeling restless and wanting out of this room. "We fought fake guards at the old prison last night. They've got a base here. Or they did."

The advisors' murmurings began again.

Lupin cut through that. "Mojek remains in the city to continue interrogations and work with our witch. If any of the slavers return to the prison, he is capable of dealing with them. We will keep you informed of any developments."

The advisors erupted again.

"Keep us informed! He can't —"

"Alphas in the city —"

"We don't take orders —"

"This is highly irregular —"

Lupin stood. "Prince Charles will act as ambassador. I require him to live in the Foreboding Forest." The big man walked out.

The Alpha had given Charlie a reason to leave the city without having to reveal his new nature. Smothering his grin, he found a poorly hidden smirk on Dashing's face. As one, they rose and walked out.

And just like that, the most efficient peace talks ever were over.

CHAPTER THIRTY ONE

FROSTINE

LUPIN, A WOLF DARK as night, and Charming, a snowy white wolf, fought one another and Dashing, who battled with his sword.

They'd barely made it out of the city. At this rate, they wouldn't get home until tomorrow. Their pace was already slow — a trail of wagons spread down the road behind them. Apparently, princes required many accouterments when they moved to a new place.

The random stops the men made to attack one another only delayed them even more. Charming needed to learn to fight, but Frostine had seen enough. She wanted to get home. Lupin had curtailed the peace talks, but there had been one detail or another to see to, as well as packing, that had taken the rest of the day.

"Petra, would you like to join me for dinner?" Frostine sighed. "The boys clearly have things to talk about. Again."

Petra rolled her eyes. "Yes. Let's go. They can travel with their wagons while we go ahead. Do you want to race?"

"I have a better idea." Frostine gave in to the calling of her winter magic and !let go of her human form. She formed a snowy whirlwind around Petra and lifted the other woman into the air.

Petra laughed as Frostine carried her away. They swept through the trees, leaving swaths of pristine snow and ice in their wake, as she shared her delight in being an elemental spirit.

When Petra showed no fear, Frostine soared into clouds high overhead. In hardly any time at all, the manor house came into view. The rock walls had lost their grimy, tired appearance and gleamed like new. The rock trolls had been at work.

Frostine set Petra on her feet in the courtyard and reformed her human self. "Come in." She pushed the front door open.

"Frostine!" All seven rock trolls crowded around them in the foyer.

She knelt to hug each one.

"You're all right!"

"Welcome back!"

"We were so worried."

"Are you home for good?"

Home for good. The words made her smile. "Yes. We've come home."

Chased from the kitchen by an indignant Stout waving a spoon, Frostine and Petra sat at the dining room table with hot drinks in newly made stone mugs.

The rock trolls had been busy turning the manor into a home. They'd used their magic to create everything from the floor, to the furniture to dishes. One by one, they brought plates and platters from the kitchen and took their places at the table. Stout joined them last, bringing a pot of stew.

Everyone helped themselves and set to eating.

"What do you want to do now?" Petra inhaled the steam from the hot cider she held.

Frostine shrugged. "We'll have to go back to the Enchanted City for the wedding at some point. Charming told everyone we're betrothed, and his parents are expecting it."

"A wedding just to Charming?" Scowly's frown deepened. "What about Dashiell?"

Dashing had earned the trolls' loyalty. "I want to marry both of them. Dashing said he doesn't mind. He doesn't like the attention, and he didn't want to rock the boat."

Petra shrugged. "So don't get married in the Enchanted City. Lupin is Alpha in the Foreboding Forest. He can perform a wedding for you and your princes. The Alphas certainly don't have a problem with untraditional. After you're all bound to each other because you chose it, who cares about ceremonies for other people later? The most important one will already be done."

"Would Lupin do that for us? Charming's hardly been a wolf for a day." Well, that and what could a man like the Alpha know about weddings?

"Charming is still a wolf. Lupin doesn't seem to have a romantic bone in his body, but he is full of surprises." Petra beamed. "You need a dress."

"The only dress I have is the one I wore to the ball." She glanced down at her traveling clothes. They were white, but pants and a tunic were hardly wedding attire. "It's packed somewhere in the wagons."

"That dress is amazing. It would work as your wedding gown. What about family? Is your father traditional, or would he come to your wedding to two men?"

In a way, Father had already bound the three of them together far more closely than a wedding. "My father knows about my relationship with the princes. He doesn't have a problem with the three of us."

"Can you get him a message?"

Frostine nodded. "On a winter breeze."

"Send it. We'll arrange everything before the boys arrive."

The rock trolls clapped their hands. "You'll need attendants. And we know just the place to have the ceremony."

"We'll need a feast." Stout headed back into the kitchen.

"Will you be my maid of honor?"

"Of course."

"And tell me what I need to know about living with a wolf?"

Petra offered an enigmatic smile as her fingers touched her neck. "How do you feel about being bitten?"

Frostine, in her mist form, hovered in the trees as Petra confronted the three men when they finally arrived in the predawn morning.

"All three of you bathe." Petra pointed at the manor house. "Frostine picked out clothes for Charming and Dashing. When you're dressed, I'll tell you what to do next."

"Where is Frostine?"

"In the forest, where she'll remain if you don't do what I say."

Grumbling, the men entered the house as the rock trolls dug through the wagons in search of her dress.

The men were ready in minutes, and while Frostine dressed, Petra escorted them to the clearing the rock trolls had chosen.

Overhead, stars and streaks of Aurora Borealis glimmered, reflected on smooth, polished black rocks on the ground, so it appeared everyone stood in the sky.

The rock trolls stood in two rows, forming an aisle. Charming and Dashing stood side by side in front of Lupin at the end.

Petra squeezed Frostine's hand, winked, and walked down the aisle, scattering snowflakes that hung in the air.

Frostine followed on her father's arm. The King of Winter handed Frostine over to her princes and stepped back. She, Dashing, and Charming faced the Alpha.

The silence went on so long Frostine had to resist the urge to fidget. Was she supposed to do something?

"Speak."

"Lupin!" Petra scolded.

He chuckled. "Frostine has invited us here this morning because, for some reason, she's agreed to wed these two men." He leaned toward her, but didn't lower his voice. "If you've come to your senses, I can hold them back long enough for you to escape."

Petra snorted and several rock trolls tittered.

Charming growled, and Dashing glared, but Frostine laughed. "I'm afraid I'm still feeling quite insensible."

"Love does that." Lupin nodded. "Very well. Have you rings?"

Frostine nodded and formed three rings of blue ice laced with silver on the palm of her upturned hand.

"And vows?"

They nodded.

Together, her princes held her ring and slipped it onto her finger.

Dashing took Frostine's hand. "I promise to give you kisses and reasons to smile every day, for the rest of my life. I love you, Frostine, and will do my best to make sure you want for nothing."

"I vow to treasure you forever." Charming took her hand and kissed her ring. "I will hold you every night, and protect you every day. You have my love, always, Frostine."

Frostine slipped a band onto the ring fingers of her princes. "I promise to love you both with the heart you helped create for me." She smiled up at each of them, marveling again at how so much had changed in only a few days. "To cherish and protect you for the rest of my life."

She gasped as a tendril of blue-silver magic streamed from her heart and split in two. One half crashed into Dashing, the other into Charming.

"Father." Frostine rubbed her chest. "What was that?"

The King of Winter stood, arms crossed, utterly unrepentant. "They vowed forever and for life. I've just made sure they can't wiggle out of their promises. They share your lifespan now. I would never have you feel the sorrow of another person you love dying, Snegurochka."

Her eyes filled with unexpected tears. "Thank you, Papa."

"I now pronounce you mates bound for life." Lupin eyed the King of Winter, who lifted an eyebrow. "In more ways than one."

As the guests clapped, the night sky turned to dawn. Sunlight streamed over the trees and snowy ground, making everything sparkle.

"The border moved." Lupin joined Petra and laced his fingers with hers. "We're officially in the Foreboding Forest now. As such, this house and the surrounding land will be your territory, Charming."

He stiffened, then relaxed. "I will make sure it is safe."

"I like it." Frostine squeezed her princes' hands. "A new land, a new day, and a new start for us."

"I'm ready to start our honeymoon." Charming's eyes gleamed silver and Dashing's darkened with lust.

"Run, Princess."

Heart light, Frostine fled toward their house.

In Dashing's bedroom, her beautiful dress proved no defense against two princes determined to have her naked. Everywhere she tried to dodge there was a hard chest, or a long arm to block her escape, and a quick hand to undress her a little more.

Frostine could have prevented the shredding of her dress with her magic, but her princes liked winning, so she let them. She would go back to Natalie and they could create more clothes. And a cloak!

The last scrap of material disappeared, leaving her clad only in icy crystals. She let her magic go, and the snowflakes began to fade.

"No!" her princes shouted together.

"Leave your magic on," Dashiell's husky voice demanded.

Charming's gray eyes glowed silver. "I want to lick it off."

A delicious shudder ran through her — at the thought of their tongues on her, but also because they accepted her completely, even though she was a wild elemental who lived in the form of a human woman.

Frostine brought her magic back, forming crystalline snowflakes on her skin.

Dashing leaned forward, closing his lips over one on her neck. Charming licked up her stomach.

Her princes groaned and moved their lips to more places, devouring her. Through her magic, their desire and love flowed to her. She filled her snowflakes with her need for them, and her love.

"I could eat these off you all night." Dashing lapped at a snowflake on her breast.

Charming sucked on her thigh. "Forget one night. I'm going to do this the rest of my life."

"Even as a big, bad wolf, he tries to be the charming one," Dashing muttered. He scooped her up, placed her on the bed, and pulled his shirt over his head.

She'd never tire of seeing Dashing's rippled stomach and chest. He popped the button on his pants and slid them down his legs. She'd never tire of seeing his muscled thighs or evidence of his lust for her, either.

Frostine eyed her other prince. Charming smiled, and pulled off his clothes. His human body had undergone some changes. Inches of corded muscle had packed onto his new, broader frame and he carried himself with more awareness of his surroundings. Her playful prince had become a predator.

Another view she'd never tire of.

Charming dipped his head to suck on a hard nipple. It tightened up almost to the point of pain. She sucked in a shuddery breath.With no warning, Dashing leaned forward and licked her clit with firm even strokes. Frostine moaned.

"I can't wait to be inside you," he whispered against the cluster of nerves, sending shock waves through her body.

Dashing sucked, increasing and decreasing his pressure and speed. Charming nipped at her breast. It all felt so perfect. She groaned again. Louder this time. Dashing slipped a finger into her slick channel. His lips moved against her clit as his finger thrust into her. It didn't take him long to find the place he was looking for. Frostine's back bowed off the bed and she whimpered.

He hummed against her clit, making her suck in a breath. Charming kept his attentions on her breasts, moving from one to the other. Frostine was all sensation, unable to discern one pleasure from another.

Dashing sucked and licked her clit thrusting deep inside her with his thick finger. "I can't wait to be inside you." He thrust faster and harder. "So tight, Little One." His finger and wicked tongue, sent her over the edge on a silent scream that ended in a loud groan.

Panting, she opened her eyes. Dashing and Charming were exchanging a look she couldn't interpret. Charming leaned forward and kissed her gently on the lips.

Charming hoisted her onto Dashing's lap so she faced him. She threaded her fingers around his neck. Her prince gave her a tight smile. "I'm going to have to think about boring things." His lips curled from his teeth as she positioned herself over his tip.

Dashing cursed softly as she slid onto him a little more. "Really, really boring and disgusting things. You do crazy things to me, Little One." He fisted her hair. "You're so beautiful. Just look at you."

She slid all the way down and he groaned, holding still for a few seconds before he moved, lifting and dropping her onto his hard, thick cock like she weighed nothing. He moved slow and carefully, keeping his eyes closed. Dashing felt so good inside her. So right.

Charming watched them with silvering eyes, his body seemed to throb every time Dashing lowered her. His neck muscles corded and his stomach muscles bunched. He snarled. For a second she was sure he was going to attack Dashing.

She reached for her Alpha. He flashed her a grin full of fangs and stepped close so she could touch him. The skin of his cock was hot and silky in her grip.

Dashing's nostrils flared and his teeth clamped together, like he was in pain. The slide of his thick length inside her made her pant. Her nipples rubbed his chest each time he lifted and lowered her.

"It's my turn." Charming narrowed his fully silver eyes as they dropped to her breasts, then to where Dashing penetrated her. He growled so low and deep, she felt the vibration even though he wasn't touching her.

With a pained sound of frustration that matched hers, Dashing lifted her off of him.

"I won't make you wait too long." Charming smiled at Dashing. "We'll both have Frostine soon."

"Both?" Frostine bit her lip.

"You won't regret it, Princess."

"We want to take you together, Little One."

"I know you want to share me, but I can't believe you both want me at the same time."

"We both want to bring you pleasure, Princess. It will be good. We'll take it slow and if it hurts, even one little bit, we'll stop. We realize you want both of us. Both of us want you. Nothing we do between the three of us is wrong."

Dashing moved to his haunches in front of her. "You know that neither of us would ever hurt you. We love you very much."

Her chest heaved as her breathing hitched. Frostine swallowed hard and nodded. Being loved by both her princes at the same time would be perfect.

CHAPTER THIRTY TWO

PRINCE CHARLES

CHARLIE MOVED TO THE edge of the bed and opened his legs. He gestured for her with both of his hands. "Sit on my lap with your back to me, Princess."

Frostine obediently came to him as he asked. He'd always loved how submissive she was, and with Alpha running in his veins, he loved her unquestioning obedience even more. He bracketed her hips with his hands, lowered her. She sighed and relaxed into him, his dick buried deep inside her.

Charming ground into her, relishing the involuntary sounds he drew from her. Her breasts jerked up and down from the force of his thrusts, but her body accepted his so eagerly, she'd already prepared him for what came next.

He eased out of Frostine's slick pussy. Her whimper at the loss sent an urge to turn her over and take her from behind through him. His nails grew sharper and dug into her skin. Time for that later.

"You play with her clit while I ease in." He kissed and nipped at her neck until she squirmed. "My cock is nice and wet with your slickness. I'll take it slow." His voice was low and husky.

"Are you ready?" Dashing eased his finger into her pussy, brought it out covered in her wetness, and slid it over her nub in slow, soft strokes.

Frostine's breathing hitched, and she managed a nod. She didn't smell scared. Her wild scent filled his nose with need.

She moaned when he put the head of his cock to her rear, and inserted the tip without too much effort. Her nipples hardened. She gasped when he eased in a little more.

Charming moved back, making a pained noise as he pushed back in, this time a little deeper than before, pressing in an inch at a time. Going so slow was going to kill him.

At long last, he sighed contentedly as he sank all the way in. "You did so well, Princess." He grunted approval and cupped one of her breasts. "So soft." He whispered against her, causing goosebumps to rise as he tweaked her nipple until she panted. He nipped at the base of her neck.

"Your turn, Dashing." He swept her hair to the side and nibbled at a snowflake on her neck, choosing the perfect place to mark her.

CHAPTER THIRTY THREE

PRINCE DASHIELL

DASHING TOOK A POSITION in front of them and kissed Frostine softly, sliding his hand down her thigh. He hooked fingers around her leg and pulled it over his hip, opening her to him.

"Take it slow." Charming's breath was on her neck, then he kissed her again, using his sharp teeth and soft lips. She moaned. It turned into an all-out groan as Dashing pushed his cock inside her. He growled. "I'm not sure we're both going to fit."

Frostine closed her eyes and her head fell back. Her mouth turned slack. "You will. I need both of you." She practically vibrated with need. Her chest heaved against his, her hard nipples teasing him.

"Take me," she pleaded to Dashing. "Please," she added when he didn't move.

His eyes heated with desire. In a smooth movement, he plunged in and was surrounded by a tight, wet vice that nearly had him coming. He gritted his teeth and pulled himself together.

"I can feel you," Dashing grunted.

"I feel you too," Charming groaned.

"I can't explain it." Dashing sighed, sliding in a little deeper, his beautiful eyes closed. "Feels good. So right."

Frostine nearly undid him when she licked at his lips, asking for him to kiss her. When he did, she lapped at him, sucking on his tongue and silently urging him to move. He rocked his hips slow, pulling back until only his tip was inside her, feeling her core suction him back, then, pushing in again in a smooth, firm motion.

Each thrust was delicious, maddening friction. She called his name, urging him to quicken his thrusts until his rhythm was an erratic pounding.

He changed his angle until the tip of his cock ground against her, causing her moans to change into frantic cries. She held on, pressing against him as she wrapped her legs around his waist, welcoming everything.

Frostine surrendering herself to him again, with such trust, shattered the last of his control. He found her pleasure point, and angled his next series of plunges there.

"I'm going to come." Dashing barely got the words out, his teeth were so tightly clenched.

CHAPTER THIRTY FOUR

FROSTINE

FROSTINE HAD NEVER felt so full. It was good but also strange. The slight burning ache never subsided but never worsened.

Dashing kept up his ministrations on her clit, but too soft, so her orgasm eluded her. She needed more and mewled a protest.

Charming chuckled. It quickly turned into a snarl as Dashing withdrew and thrust himself into her, right to the hilt. Her prince moaned as he slid in deep.

Frostine screamed in both pleasure and pain. It was too much, then her princes moved together.

Slow and gentle, the rocking motion they created seized the air in her lungs. Her clit throbbed. Every part of her seemed to come alive all at once.

Her orgasm was so close. She leaned forward allowing Charming to take her deeper and tightened her muscles around Dashing. Squeezing her eyes shut, she dug her fingers into Dashing's back as they picked up the pace.

She loved having this effect on them. All she could do was hold onto Dashing and pant and moan.

Just as her skin tightened and her pussy started to flutter with her orgasm, Charming stopped moving. He held her firmly in place with his hands on her hips. Her prince breathed heavily, and growled, the vibration went through her like lightning, and caused her to clench with need.

"I know you won't hurt me. Bite me, Charming. Mark me as yours, my Alpha."

Her sex fluttered with anticipation. The first spasms hit as she felt Charming at her neck. He ran his nose up the column of her throat and his tongue back down. Sharp teeth pierced her as he sank his fangs into her flesh.

Every nerve ending in her whole body fired at full force. Her princes held her in place as she spasmed with the intensity of her orgasm. It tore through her like a wild blizzard consuming her body.

Charming growled, body jerking against hers, and Dashing groaned as heat erupted inside her in hot bursts. Both of them kept pumping into her. Charm pushed up tightly against her, releasing her neck.

Contentment seeped through her limbs as they collapsed in a heap. Now they could start living their happily ever after.

THE END

THANK YOU

Thank you for sticking with the story to the end! If you enjoyed it, please consider leaving a review. A couple of words, or even just a rating from you can help others find my work, which will encourage me to write more stories!

ABOUT THE AUTHOR

I love to travel, read, and think of ways to complicate my characters' lives. I have two borrowed cats who take shameless advantage of my good nature. Hopefully you find my characters a lot more entertaining than I am. :)

If you enjoyed this story, you may be interested to know that I write in several series. While each novel is written for one relationship, features unique mythologies, and can be read as standalone, a little more of that world is revealed and the overall arc of the series grows throughout.

The best way to find out what's going on with the series, and me, is to visit my website at https://www.ysobellablack.com. There, you can check out the wikis and timelines for each series. Or, sign up for the newsletter.

https://ysobellablack.com/newsletter/

I send out things like surveys, freebies, contests, and random news about things going on with me that may or may not be interesting.

I love hearing from my readers. Feel free to send me an email at ysobella@ysobellablack.com.

Or find me here:

Twitter[1]

Pinterest[2]

Goodreads[3]

---

1. https://twitter.com/ysobellablack

2. https://pinterest.com/ysobellablack/

3. https://www.goodreads.com/ysobellablack

<u>Instagram</u>[4]
<u>TikTok</u>[5]
<u>Bookbub</u>[6]

---

4. https://www.instagram.com/ysobellablackauthor/

5. http://www.tiktok.com/ysobellablack

6. http://www.bookbub.com/ysobellablack

Written as Ysobel Black (Nice/Sweet Versions)

Bakery Street Cozy Mysteries

Paranormal Cozy Mysteries
The Lyrical Lycanthrope

Fairy Tales With a Twist

Retellings of fairy tales, myths, and stories you only thought you knew.
The Crimson Hood & the Alpha of Wolves
The Ice Maiden & the Princes of Diamonds

Holiday Hullabaloo

Love in Ashana can be tricky, but twelve days of chaos result in
paranormal happily-ever-afters.
A Penghou in a Pine Tree
Two Tatzelwurms
Three French Bêtes
Four Ceffyl Dŵr
Five Golden Wings
Six Grootslangs Playing

Seven Spawns a-Swimming
Eight Maenads Mixing
Nine Lazy Dragons
Ten Swords a-Sneaking
Eleven Pixie Potions
Twelve Lovers Loving

Pohjola Maidens

The Maidens of Pohjola are free, heading for the human world, and looking for love.
Dream's Sleeper: Lemminki

Strygoi Witches & Vampires

Join an Ildum of vampires over 10,000 years of history and mythology as they find their Dragăs — witches who make their hearts beat and restore their souls..
Ember's Light: Stryx
Viktoria's Shadow: Jael
Myth's Legend: Norrix
Bijou's Cure: Zeke
Musette's Fate: Idris

Strygoi Witches & Vampires Companion Stories

Shadowy — Viktoria's prequel (companion novella)
Echo's Answer: Lachlan (companion novel)

COLLECTIONS/BOX SETS

Holiday Hullabaloo
DAYS 1-12

Strygoi Witches & Vampires
COLLECTION ONE: BOOKS 1-4

Written as Ysobella Black (Naughty/Steamy Versions)

Alix in Wonderland

A reverse harem (MFMMM) retelling of Alice in Wonderland.
Madness of the Hatter

Bakery Street Mysteries

Paranormal Cozy-ish Mysteries
The Lyrical Lycanthrope

Fairy Tales With a Kink

Retellings of fairy tales, myths, and stories you only thought you knew.
The Crimson Hood & the Alpha of Wolves
The Ice Maiden & the Princes of Diamonds

Grove of Bandrui

Immortal Druids search for their Maités.
Druid of Oaks
Druid of Apples

Harom & Aneja

Witches choose three men to form their Haroms as they become
Aneja — Walkers in magic. Reverse Harem (MFMM)
RealmWalker
BeastWalker

Magical Love in London

Regency London with a paranormal twist.
Marriage of Inconvenience

Oubliette

Paranormal short and steamy stories.
Selkie
Merrow

Pohjola Passions

The Maidens of Pohjola are free, on their way to the human world,
and looking for love.
Dream's Sleeper: Lemminki

Raven Chronicles: Phoenix Rising

The battle for the Raven Throne in the Inisfail Fae Court is full of war,
sex, and intrigue that spans generations.

First Generation

Souls Lost & Found

Once in a blue moon, star-crossed lovers get a second chance for their love to shine.
The Egyptian

Utopia Pack

A pack of shifters find their Fateds.
Unyielding

Vampires & Strygoi Witches

Join an Ildum of vampires over 10,000 years of history and mythology as they find their Dragăs — witches who make their hearts beat and restore their souls.
Ember's Light: Stryx
Viktoria's Shadow: Jael
Myth's Legend: Norrix
Bijou's Cure: Zeke
Musette's Fate: Idris

Vampires & Strygoi Witches Companion Stories

Shadowy — Viktoria's Prequel
Echo's Answer: Lachlan

Xov & Xau

In a war where each side is determined to inherit the earth, sparks fly.
And when Xov finds Xau, a different sort of sparks ignite.
Poisoned Heart

Yuletide Chaos

Love in Ashana can be tricky, but twelve days of chaos result in
paranormal happily-ever-afters.
A Penghou in a Pine Tree
Two Tatzelwurms
Three French Bêtes
Four Ceffyl Dŵr
Five Golden Wings
Six Grootslangs Playing
Seven Spawns a-Swimming
Eight Maenads Mixing
Nine Lazy Dragons
Ten Swords a-Sneaking
Eleven Pixie Potions
Twelve Lovers Loving

COLLECTIONS/BOX SETS

Three First in a Series

FATED – Three Firsts

Ember's Light:Stryx
RealmWalker
Poisoned Heart

Five First in a Series

FATED – Five Firsts
Ember's Light:Stryx
The Crimson Hood & the Alpha of Wolves
RealmWalker
Dream's Sleeper: Lemminki
Poisoned Heart

Vampires & Strygoi Witches
COLLECTION ONE: BOOKS 1-4

Yuletide Yearnings
Yuletide Chaos, Days 1-12
DAYS 1-12

www.ingramcontent.com/pod-product-compliance
Lightning Source LLC
Chambersburg PA
CBHW031155160726
PP18580100001B/1